I0710467

MARS, THE BAND MAN, AND SARA SUE

L. MARIE WOOD

MOCHA MEMOIRS PRESS

COPYRIGHT NOTICE

The story contained therein are works of fiction. Names, characters, places, and incidents are products of the authors' imagination or are used fictitiously and are not to be construed as real. Any resemblance to actual events, locales, organizations, or persons, living or dead, is entirely coincidental.

ISBN: 978-1-962353-08-3

Copyright©2002 L. Marie Wood

Cover Art by S.H. Roddey

Former Editor: Laura Fasching and Michael Wood

Proofreader: Novellette Whyte

Publisher: Mocha Memoirs Press

All rights reserved. No part of this book may be used or reproduced electronically or in print without written permission, except in the case of brief quotations embodied in reviews. Due to copyright laws, you cannot trade, sell or give any e-books away.

OTHER L. MARIE WOOD TITLES

Acknowledgments

Thank you, Sean, Bree, and Mike, for helping me find pockets of time to do this thing I love.

Thank you, Laura Fasching, for your keen eyes along this journey.

Thank you, readers, for travelling along this road with me.

This one's for my girls. You know who you are.

CHAPTER 1

Cute.

That's the word he used to describe her. Not *beautiful*, or *sexy*, or any of the adjectives she would have rather heard. *Cute* is what he said. Actually, he said, "You're the cutest."

Puppies and kittens are cute. Baby monkeys and small animals. Infants. Pants. Shoes. Those things are cute. She wanted to be more than that—more than just something nice to look at. She wanted to be someone that people couldn't *stop* looking at.

To most people, she was fine—average. Nothing to jump up and down about but nothing to turn away from either. Just Sara Sueantha Prentis—Sara Sue for short—your everyday, middle-class chickadee, diamond studs and pedicure included. And they were right. But in her mind, she was earthy, gritty—one of those wannabe-rock-band-members-but-can't-read-music type of people. Sara Sue wanted to be different in a cool kind of way. She wanted to stand out... but she didn't. She hated it, but damn it, she was more than just cute.

The "he" Sara Sue was talking about was her husband Charlie, the mechanic. She had never expected him to be a mechanic. It was not the mechanic part that bugged her—a paying job was always a good thing. It was just that at one time, early in their relationship, Charlie had a real shot at being great, and all that was washed away in an instant. That he took his place in the family business without blinking also pissed her off. It was then that she had started to hate him, Sara Sue realized, all those years ago.

Charlie was supposed to go off to college to make something of himself with the football scholarship he had earned, but all of that changed senior year. Charlie the mechanic, then the All-American quarterback and most popular boy at Cherry Blossom High, had gotten sacked in one of the last games of the season. He had gone down, cracking his head so hard on the ground that the sound of it echoed up to the bleachers. The hit had detached both his retinas and broken his skull; this had taken him out of the game forever and had deposited him directly into his father's garage where he learned to be a grease monkey.

Sara Sue hadn't had to marry him, she always reminded herself of that when she thought about how his hair was thinning and how he whistle-snored the moment his head hit the pillow all the way through to the next morning when he got up for work. She had a choice back then, and she had decided to become Mrs. Prentis. Why? Because she had loved what being with Charlie did for her. He had owned the school, and because she was with him, people had treated her with a sort of deference she wouldn't have gotten otherwise. Sure, she had been a cheerleader (how stereotypical is that?) and she'd gotten her fair share of attention, but not like Charlie. He had been like a god to the folks around town; all they had was high school football and barbeque sauce competitions, so seeing Charlie go down had been like watching Walter Payton retire from the NFL. And he had been hot back then. Sara Sue had wanted to be on the arm of the best-looking guy her little burb had ever seen. She hadn't been ready to give all that up, even if her dreams of mansions and money were dashed by some idiot sophomore from a school two towns over.

After Charlie's accident, Sara Sue had thrown herself into looking after him. That had made her look good, too—the dedicated girlfriend doting on her fallen boyfriend. It had also given her something to do once high school was finished, at least in the short term. Then he had asked her to marry him, and Sara Sue had felt butterflies in her stomach. Yeah, she had loved Charlie too. Still did, she hoped.

But on this particular day she wasn't thinking about her love for Charlie or how hot he still was. She was wondering how the beautiful cheerleader with a gazillion friends and perky tits had ended up being just *cute* 20 years later, and it was a few more years than that if she was being honest. She also wondered why the hell it bothered her so much.

What was wrong with her?

Sara Sue looked into her eyes in the rearview mirror and squinted as she tried to remember how long she had felt disenchanted or if she had ever felt "enchanted" in the first place.

Sara Sue shifted her gaze to look at the road, the tree-lined street, the kids playing on the sidewalk. *It's nice*, she thought, the life she and Charlie had made for themselves. For all the things that had worn thin about Charlie, he was still a decent provider. Sara Sue didn't have to work, and that was fine by her. Charlie was okay with her not working because neither of them wanted to send their children to daycare... that is, whenever they had children. Sara Sue didn't know if she wanted to have children anymore. She couldn't imagine being responsible for another life—she could hardly get her own life together. So, Sara Sue went to yoga and step classes instead of clocking in at a job. She drank coffee from Starbucks and shopped. She didn't volunteer, didn't do anything part-time to bring in money. She clipped coupons and cooked dinner most nights. That was enough.

The passion was gone. Charlie tried, but Sara Sue didn't think he *could* give her what she wanted. The butterflies-in-the-stomach passion, the can't-do-without-you glances over the dinner table. That was just not happening anymore. When Sara Sue tried to liven things up a bit, give him the looks she wanted to get from him, Charlie didn't respond in kind. To most people, that kind of affection wasn't necessary, but it was for Sara Sue. She wanted it. Badly.

Sara Sue laid on the horn out of frustration. The car in front of her took a left turn slowly, even more slowly after being beeped at it seemed. Sara Sue felt like getting out of the car and popping the driver—some soccer mom with a Gap sweater sitting on the passenger seat and a Bluetooth earpiece glowing in her ear—but she didn't. Sara Sue wasn't mad at her. She wasn't mad at Charlie either. Sara Sue was mad at herself. This wasn't the life she wanted. This normal, suburban life with cookie-cutter houses outfitted with the best in alarm systems and other techie gadgets, perfectly trimmed shrubs, and green lawns. Sara Sue's hot pink toenails and pink striped sandals stood out; they screamed, "Hey! Look at me!" Her trendy city-girl heart was dying in captivity.

She wanted to be Sara Sue the artist whose work was actually taken seriously at galleries; Sara Sue the poet whose poems had moved so many people to tears that her spoken-word gigs were always sold out; Sara Sue the model, wildly successful in the US and abroad, who made curviness the norm rather than being the next candidate for full-figure ads; Sara Sue the trendsetter whose every fashion decision was pondered over by talking heads and replicated by young people everywhere—not Sara Sue the socialite who could hold a balanced tree pose in yoga class.

Ridiculous. The whole damned thing.

Sara Sue was positive she was straddling the line between reality and hopeless insanity now.

Sara Sue pounded the steering wheel to jar her mind out of her reconstruction fantasy, deciding it was better to save herself from her rapid-fire thoughts than to sink into them, but they just wouldn't go away. Instead, they hung in the air, baiting her to watch them play like a movie reel.

Sara Sue didn't give in because she knew how that particular movie went. And as she was with everything else, Sara Sue was bored with the plot.

Sara Sue wheeled her convertible into the mall parking lot, slid into a space, and hopped out. She walked to the door slowly—she was in no rush. She wasn't going to the mall for anything in particular; she was just planning to browse. Another boring thing to do, but it was either that or sit in front of the television watching soap operas all day. That might just kill her.

The mall was full of kids; some hanging out, some shopping with their Mommy's credit cards. She strolled toward one of the stores geared toward young-adult girls and stood at the doorway looking at the swarm of pencil-sized women picking through the clothes. She felt silly going inside; she'd never find anything in her size, considering that a size 6 in a store like that was really a size 10 in department stores. But worse, she felt old even looking through the window.

Sara Sue walked to the other end of the mall and chose the music store as a viable second option. She picked through the CDs looking for something new, but she didn't want any rap or metal, folk or jazz. Hip hop, maybe, but only if there wasn't a rapper on every tune. That alone made her old, not of this generation, past her musical prime. Sara Sue tried to listen to radio stations that played contemporary music—the stuff the kids liked—but she couldn't get most of it down. The rap sounded so angry, and she honestly couldn't tell the difference between rap and R&B anymore. That left her with what people called "oldies" ... music from when she was a kid and decidedly not old at all. At least not to Sara Sue. She flipped through CDs from the 80s, a terrible truth becoming clearer by the second. Maybe she *wasn't* as daring as she thought she was. Maybe she really *was* as boring as she seemed and her life was actually the way it was supposed to be. Maybe, just maybe, this really was *it* for her; maybe she was just a suburban chick, like it or lump it. Slowly falling into a funk, Sara Sue flipped through the CDs in alphabetical order ABBA (did they even *have* any new music?), Amelia, Ash (whoever they were), more names she didn't recognize. Nothing jumped out at her until she got to the Ls.

Lover.

Sara Sue stared at the cover, a kitschy cartoon heart with a picture of the band in the middle blowing kisses at the camera, the title *To Love You* printed across the top. In some part of her mind, she knew the cover looked ridiculous, a throwback to the early 80s when neon anything and white knee boots were just starting to be considered cool, but she couldn't pull her eyes away. She saw the perfectly styled hair and the made-up cheeks, and on the rest of the band, it looked as ridiculous as their outfits did. But on the lead singer it looked incredible.

Perfect.

Right.

It was a compilation CD with only ten tracks on it. Sara Sue couldn't remember four of their songs, let alone ten, but the music didn't matter. There was another photo on the back of the CD. All feathered hair and glossy lips. Memories of the pink walls in her bedroom covered with posters and *New York Hot Tracks* videos on television flooded in. Sara Sue felt like she had stepped into another world—a familiar world filled with half gloves and Jheri-curled hair, spiked arm bracelets and two-toned pants. She remembered watching Lover on the MTV music awards, remembered how they toggled between sneering at the camera and making goo-goo eyes at it. Sara Sue was smiling—she could feel her cheeks flushing too—but she couldn't stop herself. If anyone turned around and saw what she was holding in her hand, she would be branded ancient for sure.

Sara Sue looked at the CD cover again, closer this time. It was silly, really, when you looked at it. A bunch of men dressed in sexually ambiguous clothing with too much makeup on and hair that was just too… big. But there was something about the one guy, the lead, that drew her attention, grabbed it, and held it captive. It was like he was looking at her from the CD cover, communicating with his eyes. She knew that was ridiculous, but she couldn't deny the feeling it gave her, the warm burn in the pit of her stomach. Girls always liked the lead singer in groups, right? That's what it was, she told herself. That's what it had to be.

The lead singer was tall and slim; his understated muscles were covered by a ridiculous lace top that no self-respecting woman would be caught wearing in the 2000s. Though softened by makeup and cleaned of any trace of facial hair, his features were strong. His chin drew a distinctive line, defining the strength of his face. Sara Sue found herself wondering how his face looked when his jaw worked to form words. A little dimple in one of his cheeks maybe? His full lips, unsmiling in his attempt to look cool, pouted just a little. His nostrils flared, hinting at an ethnic quality in him that she liked. He stood with his head downturned, as though pensive. He looked at the camera like she imagined he might look at a woman he was trying to seduce, his eyelids lowered, peeking through his eyelashes, mischief dancing in his light brown irises. Those eyes. Sara Sue felt like she could fall right into them. If seduction was the goal, it was certainly working.

Sara Sue tried to remember his name but couldn't. She tried to remember the name of the band's song that was all over the radio during her senior year. Something about wanting to "feel good all over." The one part she kept hearing in her mind could have come from countless songs by any number of groups—she could easily be combining two or three of them. But again, it didn't matter. He was speaking to her from the cover of the CD—his eyes saying everything she needed to know. With no listening section in sight, she took the CD to the cashier and paid for it.

Sara Sue walked the mall a little longer, trying to suppress the urge to run to the car so she could put her new CD on. It was odd, this starstruck thing she was indulging in. She hadn't looked at an actor or singer with anything more than mild interest since she was in high school, but the lead singer of Lover really made her look twice. Should she run to a pay phone and squeal with her girl-friends?

Sara Sue decided to go to the bookstore and look through the magazine rack at the front of the store. She didn't want to admit that she was looking for any mention of Lover, but she was. *Are they still performing?* she wondered. If they were, would they be anywhere near here? Maybe she could get Charlie to take her to the concert. He'd think it was silly but he'd go. She would bring that old pair of binoculars she had and would train them on the lead singer—see if he was still good-looking. But there was no mention of Lover in any of the magazines, no new CDs, no tour dates—not even at the venues that had oldies gigs (it made her sick to think of herself that way, but that's what society said she was. Over thirty equals oldie. Mid-twenties equals hottie.)

She left the mall after wasting twenty minutes flipping through magazines. By the time she sat down on the convertible's hot leather seats, the CD was burning a hole in her hand.

Sara Sue advanced the CD, skipping through songs after only a couple of seconds, looking for the one that she remembered. She found it; it was the second to last song on the CD.

Everyday... I see you walking by... and I wonder if I... I... I could make you... feel good all over... yeah, I said I want to do it good all over...

Sara Sue could feel the grin on her face and knew she looked like a world-class loser sitting in her car blasting tunes from almost 15 years ago.

Sara Sue looked at the CD cover again, opened it, and scanned for the lead singer's name.

Troy Phillips.

Of course!

She and her friends had swooned over him for a little while, just before New Edition came back out sans Bobby Brown and took their attention away. She was alive back then. Carefree. She longed for times like those again—times when none of the monotony of life had set in yet and everything still looked like fun after you turned 21.

Sara Sue sighed. This was how it always started. Somehow, someway, things made her think about the lackluster life she had. She's only been with one man her whole life—she hadn't even kissed another guy before Charlie. She was fifteen when she had her first kiss. She and Charlie had been in the deep end of the pool. He'd kissed her and she'd kissed him back. It was weird; his tongue had been slimier than she'd thought it would be, but she had still liked it. It all happened so fast. Charlie had smiled and she had melted. He leaned in, opened his mouth, put it on hers, played tag with her tongue. And then it was over. She hadn't thought he'd kiss her again; she'd thought maybe she had done it wrong, but he'd asked her to go to the movies the next day and had been kissing her ever since.

How incredibly boring.

The CD player blasted Lover's singsongy ballad and she made an effort to listen, to pull herself away from the edge of self-pity and back to the sound of the lead singer's voice. His voice was melodic, she could honestly say that much. He could carry a tune and seemed comfortable begging to be touched and kissed. Soon she became comfortable hearing it, internalizing the words, imagining them being whispered in her ear.

I want to do it good all over...

Sara Sue could almost believe he really did want to do it good all over... to her. As the song went on, she imagined him in front of her, telling her what he wanted, singing it to her just like he did on the record, but this time without music backing him up: a cappella. He was alone and vulnerable. He wanted Sara Sue more than he had ever wanted anyone in his life. He wanted to do it good all over.

Sara Sue chuckled nervously, sure someone would see her

sitting there, caught up in a ridiculous fantasy, her eyes shut and a stupid grin plastered on her face.

She opened her eyes and looked around the parking lot. She didn't see anyone looking back, but she felt as if someone was. Sara Sue pulled down the sun visor and snapped open the mirror, trying to look busy. She looked at herself, expecting to see the beginnings of a blush popping up on her cheeks, and she was right. Sara Sue sighed but didn't have the urge to look away. The color on her cheeks made her look different, more alive. The blush brought out her eyes, the pinkish tones in her skin. For the first time in she couldn't remember how long, Sara Sue thought she looked good. Better than good. Beautiful.

Heels clacked against the asphalt sounding like they were right outside her car door, pulling her attention away from her reflection. Sara Sue turned to see a woman walking close to her car, oblivious of her sitting there. The woman's long brown hair was parted in the middle and fell just past her shoulders. It was bone straight and highlighted with a soft, muted blonde. Her skirt was short, very short, but she could pull it off because her legs were long. Her face was oval and she had features similar to Sara Sue's own.

The girl was looking in the opposite direction from where Sara Sue sat gawking at her. That's what Sara Sue was doing, she had to admit.

Staring.

She was enthralled.

The girl was beautiful with her button nose and full, shapely lips. Her eyes were also oval, her eyebrows trimmed in beautiful arches. A hint of a smile played on her mouth, as though she had a private joke running through her mind. Sara Sue wanted that same smile on her own lips, wanted to be that coy, that mysterious. The more she looked at the girl, the more she realized that she wanted to be like her.

The girl passed by and Sara Sue craned her neck to watch her walk away. Her gait was peppy but not bouncy; she walked on the balls of her feet. There was a little bit of a swish, her behind swaying beneath her skirt, but just a little. This girl—Michelle, Sara Sue decided she would call her (she didn't know why, but the name worked)—didn't need to shake her bottom to make people look at her. Michelle commanded attention just because of the way she looked, the freshness of her face.

Sara Sue appreciated Michelle's shape until she got into her car, a black Pontiac Sunfire convertible. A woman with similar tastes to her own. As the girl drove away, Sara Sue rounded out her personality in her head. She was young, sexy, sassy. She did what she wanted and didn't take any crap from anyone. This girl—Michelle—was the embodiment of the make-believe girl Sara Sue fancied herself to be. Sara Sue put her car in reverse and backed out of the parking spot without realizing it. She found herself behind the Sunfire at the light.

On purpose?

Probably.

Sara Sue wasn't ready for the fantasy to end.

Sara Sue turned down her radio and listened to what Michelle was playing: music emanated from her car. Some sort of rap/rock combo with incoherent lyrics. Michelle couldn't be more than twenty-two, so it made sense that she would be listening to something like that. The music Sara Sue could do without, but she couldn't seem to pull her eyes away from Michelle, her car, the whole package. Sara Sue studied Michelle as she laid her head against the headrest and combed her hands through her hair, waiting for the light to change. She was sensuous, even performing the most basic of movements. Michelle seemed to possess a knowledge of herself that few women ever did, and Sara Sue envied her for it. Michelle was confident. Michelle was sexy. Sara Sue felt more drawn to her than she did to anything or anyone else in her life.

Sara Sue watched Michelle pull a lanyard with a badge

attached to it over her head and lay it on the passenger seat. She must work in the mall. Sara Sue vowed she would be back the next day to try to find her. She wanted more—she wanted to hear Michelle's voice, watch Michelle in action. Sara Sue was sure she could learn from her, pattern herself after the young woman in some ways. She was looking for a change, and the catalyst had just fallen in her lap.

A loud beep snapped Sara Sue out of her daydream. Michelle and the little black Sunfire were gone, and the light had already turned yellow.

CHAPTER 2

Sara Sue drove the familiar streets leading to her house the way she had every day for ten years, but they seemed different now. That she was able to get home on autopilot didn't bother her; Sara Sue had something else piquing her interest.

Sara Sue pulled into her driveway thinking of how Michelle's skirt hugged her tight little behind, a behind Sara Sue used to have too and would have again if all the exercise she was putting in worked the way it was supposed to. Sara Sue wanted skirts to fit her that way. She wanted her legs to look as shapely as Michelle's did.

Lover played loudly, filling up the inside of the convertible as Sara Sue closed the top. She had no intention of bringing the CD into the house. She didn't want to share Troy with Charlie.

Sara Sue stayed in the car after shutting off the engine, her thoughts dancing between Michelle's swaying hips and Troy's beautiful eyes. She imagined his eyes watching those hips, but those hips being hers and not Michelle's. Sara Sue thought of Troy looking at the beauty mark on her left butt cheek: one of the few things she still loved about her body. She thought of Troy's fingers reaching out to caress that spot, leaning in to kiss it. Sara Sue licked her lips, her tongue feeling hot as it touched her skin.

"You gonna sit there all day?"

Charlie's voice pulled her away from her daydream, jarring her, forcing her back into her boring, run-of-the-mill life.

"Sara Sue?"

Charlie was smiling. He'd come home early probably wanting to have sex. He had been doing that a lot lately—part of his effort to make a change in their relationship. Sara Sue put on a smile as she got out of the car hoping it made her look like she was happy to see him.

"I came home early," Charlie started, stating the obvious. It took everything she had not to say, "Is that so?"

"I was hoping maybe we could..."

His giggle sounded so much like a pig snorting it made Sara Sue wrinkle her nose.

She couldn't respond.

She was afraid to open her mouth, afraid that her words might betray her.

Instead, she smiled a little harder and walked past him. She took the steps up to the house slowly, knowing he was watching. Once she reached the door, she looked back at him and winked.

As Sara Sue darted into their split-level house, ran up the stairs, and made her way across the living room and down the hall to the master bedroom, listening all the while to Charlie's heavy steps bounding through the house in pursuit, his grumbling audible as he turned off the alarm she had left for him to disengage, she thought of Michelle and her little behind and the way it might look running through a room. She thought of Troy and his beautiful eyes watching that behind as it moved. She heard Troy's voice, not Charlie's, as she lay down and opened the top button of her pants.

"Baby, I've been thinking about this all day," was what Charlie uttered as he pawed at Sara Sue's breasts and buried his face in the crevice formed by her neck and shoulder, lips roaming, tongue flicking. She heard the same words Charlie said, but in her head, they were a bit higher in pitch, sung over a delicate melody. *This* became *you*, and what was once a song became a whisper repeated over and over and over.

Baby, I've been thinking about you all day.

Baby, I've been thinking about you all day.

Baby, I've been thinking about you all day.

"Yeah," she whispered, "So have I."

CHAPTER 3

Sara Sue woke up and started her day on a mission. It was finally time to make a change, to do something different; if she didn't, she was going to lose her mind. Her life followed the same path most days—she got up early, read the paper, waited for Charlie to get up, made breakfast, went out to find something to fill the hours with, talked to a friend on the phone and heard about her equally boring life. Then Charlie would come home hungry, they'd watch a movie, have sex, and go to sleep. Day after day after day. Something had to change; that something was Sara Sue.

And what better day for change than today?

She got dressed, feeling excited about what she had planned. She was going back to the mall to find Michelle, to watch her, to see what she was like. She didn't want to *become* Michelle, but thought that dressing like her, maybe emulating a couple of her qualities, might do the trick. Just a little something. A little spice.

"Today is the first day of the rest of your life," Sara Sue said aloud as she locked her front door.

Kickboxing class, a stop at the post office, and lunch with her girlfriend Karen all came before her trip to the mall. Lunch went longer than she expected; Karen wanted Sara Sue's help taking a flattering picture for her profile on one of those online dating sites. Karen's divorce was pending—there was no turning back now, and she didn't want to even if she could. She was ready to hit the dating scene and hit it hard. After lunch, they took pictures of Karen at the marina in front of boats to piggyback on the description of her hobbies that she had posted on the site: "loves scuba diving and sailing." Sara Sue took pictures of Karen looking away from the camera at a field of what Sara Sue thought were pretty weeds but Karen insisted were wild morning daisies. They then drove forty-five minutes to the city just to take four pictures— Karen laughing with a frothy coffee drink carefully placed on the bistro table in front of her; Karen in the park, then on a busy side-walk; Karen, coming out of a trendy clothing store deliberately not looking at the camera. Karen said she felt like a model on a photo shoot. Sara Sue felt like an ass holding a digital camera.

Karen had been so excited after playing model for the day that she had left the camera on the backseat of Sara Sue's car when they got back to their little town. Sara Sue put it in the glove compart-ment so no one would see it while she was in the mall. God forbid, if someone stole the thing, they'd have to do another photo shoot with a new camera. Sara Sue didn't relish the thought of that.

Sara Sue ended up getting to the mall at the same time the junior high school girls were getting dropped off by their mothers. She had turned off the Lover CD while Karen was in the car. Even though Karen wouldn't have thought it was weird for her to be listening to throwback music, that she would consider it throw-back in the first place annoyed Sara Sue, and she just hadn't felt like dealing with it. Karen was thirty-one. Far enough in age from Sara Sue's to make a distinction, to call out the difference. Twenty years ago, Karen would have been eleven years old. Her memories of Lover would have been sandwiched between cotton candy and monkey bars.

As Sara Sue was turning into the mall parking lot, the newscast shifted to something that interested her more than she thought it would.

"Stargazers and dreamers alike will get an eyeful next week. Mars is expected to be visible in the early morning hours of August 27. The red planet, fourth from the sun, will be closer to its nearest neighbor, Earth, than it has ever been. You'd better pull that old telescope out of the attic because this is a once-in-a-lifetime experience—Mars won't be this close to Earth again for another 60,000 years."

Sara Sue coasted into a parking spot with a smile spreading across her face.

This was perfect.

This was the perfect time to do something with her life—even the stars and the planets were aligned for something big.

August 27—that gave her a little less than a week. That was enough time to make the change, to transform herself into someone who was flashy, hot, cool. Without a timeline, Sara Sue would have sat and twiddled her thumbs, but now she had a goal. She had a plan.

And Mars was going to make its debut right alongside her.

Sara Sue got out of the car and bounded toward the mall, a new spring in her step. She made her way to the clothing store she had hesitated in front of the day before and went inside. Racks were filled with low-rider jeans, and baby doll tees dotted the racks, making the pathway between them feel more like a slalom than a straight line. Belts, costume jewelry, and hats in all colors and styles bordered the chaotic center. Mannequins done up in the latest styles stood in the window in suggestive poses. Pictures of men and women papered the walls—boys and girls, really... none of them looked older than nineteen, and that was pushing it—the men with their shirts off and their abs ripping, the women wearing crop tops and showing off their midriffs. Sara Sue took a deep breath and turned her attention to a rack toward the back. If she was going to do this, she wanted some measure of privacy. She would die if one of her oh-so-perfect neighbors strolled by and saw her in a store that catered to young adults and women in their thirties who were trying to recapture their youth... like she was.

Sara Sue waded through shirts that looked too small to fit a nine-year-old and pants with sequins, or embroidery, or handprints. Pants that looked more like pajama bottoms. Who wore that stuff? She was starting to think she had made a mistake when she saw Michelle walk into the store. Michelle was wearing brown pinstripe low riders that fit snuggly but not obscenely and a cream mesh top over a cream spaghetti strap shell. She looked natural in her clothes, like she was *supposed* to be in them. Her outfit was trendy without looking like she was trying too hard. And her ass sure looked nice in those pants.

The girl behind the counter started talking to Michelle while Sara Sue milled around, borderline creeping. Sara Sue wondered what size Michelle's pants where, what kind of underwear she wore—it had to be thongs because she couldn't see a panty line. She wondered if Michelle always dressed so nicely or if she was just dressed for work. Sara Sue was aware that she was starting to obsess and she didn't like it, but she couldn't do anything to stop it either. Michelle captivated her.

Then all of a sudden, Michelle was gone.

Sara Sue must have zoned because she hadn't seen Michelle leave the store. When she looked up, Michelle was already out in the mall, almost completely past the store window. Sara Sue didn't know when she had made the decision to follow Michelle, but she definitely had; she found herself walking out of the store fast before Michelle could get too far out of sight. Sara Sue weaved through the growing crowd, trying to stay close but not too close. Michelle walked into a store that Sara Sue had never paid much attention to. It was another clothing store, but one a little more geared to adults than the one she had just suffered through. It had the same kind of clothing—capris, jeans, graphic tees—yet designs made for older people, a little more muted... more refined. Browns and blues painted the display window instead of neon yellows and greens. Sara Sue could find what she was looking for there, she was sure of it.

She watched Michelle walk into the store and do something behind the counter. So, this is where she worked. It made sense—the same brown pants Michelle was wearing were on the rack in front of the store. A smile crossed Sara Sue's lips as she made her way to the rack to get a closer look. She pulled one leg out, checking out the pinstripe and wondering if she could actually pull them off.

"I love 'em," a voice behind her said, "but I guess that's obvious, huh?"

Sara Sue turned around to see Michelle standing behind her, smiling. Her teeth were perfect and her smile lit up her face. She was taller than Sara Sue—noticeably so. Her shoulders were thinner and so was her waist—considerably thinner. They were different in so many ways but the same in one. Sara Sue's hair matched Michelle's. They had chosen the same color.

It was kismet.

Sara Sue knew she should say something back or else she would look silly. She struggled to find something hip to say, some current comeback like, "Yeah, they're banging" or "hot" or something, but she couldn't settle on one. She didn't want to seem dated, so she nodded instead.

"I bet they'll look good on you," Michelle said, speaking again. "You should definitely try them on."

Is she trying to make nice, be a good salesperson for her cutesy little company, or does she really think they would look good on me? Sara Sue wondered. Michelle was flashing her "Don't worry, I don't get commission—I'm just here to help" smile. Sara Sue didn't know if she should believe that smile or not, but she was having a good time getting an eyeful of the girl's style.

"And you could put this with it," Michelle said while taking the same top she was wearing off a rack behind Sara Sue, "and we'd be twins!"

Michelle laughed again; the sound was melodic and light. Sara Sue laughed right along with her.

"Maybe I will," Sara Sue said, finding her voice. "Thanks."

"Excellent. What size top do you wear?"

The question was innocent enough, but it sent waves of fear through Sara Sue. She wasn't big by any means. She knew rationally she had nothing to be ashamed of, but this girl was thin in the way that only twenty-year-olds can be. She didn't look like she had to work out to keep her figure—it looked natural. Michelle probably never had to wonder if the size 4s she pulled from the rack would fit or if she would have to go up to a 6. Sara Sue, on the other hand, deliberated between the size 10 she knew she should fit in or the size 12 that would be more comfortable. She thought if she had to admit out loud that she needed a large top she would bolt out of the store and never look back.

"Tina? Can you help me up here?" the girl at the register asked.

Michelle excused herself politely, but not before she handed Sara Sue the top she had selected. Sara Sue let out a sigh of relief so loud she was sure the people around her heard it. Sara Sue quickly sorted through the pants and tops, looking for her sizes, just in case Michelle came back sooner rather than later. As she made her way to the dressing room with two pairs of the pants (a size 10 *and* a size 12) and a large top, she tried to look like she had been in the store before—like she belonged there.

So, her name is Tina, Sara Sue thought. Tina. It didn't really fit her. It was too old. She decided she would stick to calling her Michelle. It suited her. Foxy, young, and sophisticated Michelle.

The pants—the 10s—actually looked pretty good. She liked the combination of the pants and top on herself as much as she liked it on Michelle. Sara Sue stood in the mirror, striking several different poses that showed off her behind, her waistline, the little bit of cleavage you could see through the mesh. She let her hair down to rest on her shoulders, then she pulled it up and let wisps drift down on the sides and back. Yeah, she looked good. Damn good.

This was the kind of outfit that would turn heads. Charlie's head would spin for sure. If he could see her, she knew Troy would do a double take too.

Sara Sue came out with one pair of pants and the top, leaving the other one in the dressing room. The girl who was at the register was gone and Michelle's smiling face greeted her.

"Looks like the outfit works for you, too!" Michelle's hands deftly pulled the clothes off the hangers and folded them as she spoke.

Sara Sue smiled and nodded, feeling tongue-tied.

"Well, I know you'll love them," Michelle said, her voice perky, but not annoying. She leaned in conspiratorially and said, "The guys really like these pants."

Sara Sue laughed because she knew she was supposed to do something, but Michelle's words caught her off guard. Why was this girl speaking to her so much? Had Michelle caught her looking? Maybe she thought Sara Sue was interested in her, as in "let's go out on a date" interested. Sara Sue straightened her shoulders and leaned back a bit. She had to make sure Michelle didn't get the wrong idea. As disinterested in Charlie as she may be, she wasn't ready to switch teams just yet.

When Michelle was done bagging and Sara Sue had paid for her clothes, she started out of the store. She was happy. She had gotten what she came for and was ready to try it out in her world. She also felt a little self-conscious—she could feel Michelle watching her as she left.

"Have a nice day!" Michelle called from the counter. Sara Sue couldn't bring herself to turn around, to respond at all.

Sara Sue fooled around the mall, going into stores and looking for outfits similar to what she had already bought. She found a couple in the larger department stores, and even though they cost a little more, she decided to go for it. This was a makeover; she was allowed to splurge a little.

Sara Sue ducked her head into the lingerie store in search of something sexy. Charlie always said that lingerie was worthless since it was just going to come off anyway, but she like it. She like the way it felt against her skin, the way she looked in it. She liked being sexy. And since she had decided it was time for her to think about herself, she decided she would pick up a little something lacy.

After the lingerie store, she stopped by the makeup counter in one of the department stores and went with a more earthy palate than she usually wore. The girl behind the counter, who was wearing a little too much makeup for her taste, told Sara Sue that the pinkish lip gloss she was wearing was in the wrong color family for her skin. That Sara Sue had never thought of what color family she should be using was evident—none of the lipstick colors she had ever worn were in the earth tones group... in fact, they were all over the map. Sara Sue got a makeover right then and there and, even though she ended up with a little more rouge on than she would normally wear even when, on the rare occasions, she was going out for a night on the town, she looked great. Better than great. She looked fantastic.

Sara Sue made a couple of other stops in the mall: she got some new shoes and a purse; she picked up a flyer about teeth whitening; and she got her hair highlighted by a real hair stylist instead of doing it herself with some $3.99 boxed product she found on the shelf at Walmart. She was feeling great about herself for the first time in a long time.

More than once her thoughts drifted to Charlie and what he would think about all of this. He would probably like the makeup and probably the hair too. She wondered what he would think about the clothes. She wanted him to like them, to like everything she had done that day, but she didn't know why. She seemed to go between caring about Charlie's opinions and not giving a shit what he thought. Why was that? Was it him? Was it her? Was this part of the boredom that had overtaken her? Maybe things would change with the new and improved Sara Sue. But change how?

CHAPTER 4

It was late when Sara Sue left the mall—9:00 p.m., almost closing time. She chuckled to herself as she walked to her car sitting almost by itself in the parking lot. She hadn't intended to stay in the mall that long, but it was worth it. No harm no foul: Charlie wasn't home and wouldn't be for hours—his poker game was probably just getting good.

She popped the trunk and threw in her bags. As she slid into the front seat and got ready to unlatch the convertible top, she saw a familiar figure in the rearview mirror. Michelle. She was walking toward her car.

Perfect timing.

Something inside her tingled, kind of flipped, like when she was a teenager pining for Corey Haim in *The Lost Boys*. She wanted to get out of the car and show herself off. She wanted to say, *"Now I'm hot, too."*

She waited until Michelle turned her car on before turning over her own engine and following her out of the parking lot, forgetting all about taking her top down. A right and left later, Sara Sue was still behind her, passing by her own turn and following Michelle wherever she was going. Sara Sue hadn't intended on tailing her, but that's exactly what she was doing. She was intrigued by the girl for some reason and wasn't ready to say good night yet. So, where was Michelle going? A girl like her couldn't possibly end the night at 9 o'clock. That was for old married people. Prudes. People like her.

Sara Sue saw Michelle tap something in her ear and cock her head to the side—she must be wearing an earpiece. Sara Sue settled into her ride, going faster than usual to keep pace with Michelle as she sped along the residential street. The realization that she was stalking a girl who didn't know her from Adam played at the corners of her mind. What would she say if the police stopped her? *I'm trying to catch up with the girl in that black Sunfire up ahead, Officer. I just want to see where she's going.*

Michelle turned off the residential street abruptly and pulled into the lot of a community park. She slid into a space next to a dark-colored coupe. Sara Sue decided not to follow her into the park—that would look way too obvious. But she wasn't ready for the night to end. As pathetic as it was, this was the most action she had seen all month.

Sara Sue slowed down, passing the two cars. She scoured the street for a place to pull in and watch, not knowing why she wanted to anymore. She had originally followed Michelle to find out where she hung out. As ridiculous as it sounded, that was the truth. But now, when it was clear that Michelle wasn't going to some trendy club, Sara Sue knew she should be turning her car around and heading home. What she was doing was the definition of eavesdropping, minding someone else's business, stalking, and she should call it quits. But she didn't want to. What Sara Sue wanted was to watch what was about to happen. She knew that was nosy and absolutely wrong, but that didn't change the fact that she was going to do it.

She turned off her Lover CD—her theme music, as she had taken to thinking of it—and turned onto the street just past the park, one that doubled back in the direction they had come from. It was lined with older houses, some in good shape, some on their last legs, just like most of the communities in the area... like her own. She could have just as easily pulled onto the street she grew up on. About halfway down the street, she turned off her lights and made a three-point turn she hoped went unnoticed by Michelle and whoever was in the other car. She navigated her car to a stop under the branches of an overhanging tree in front of a paint-chipped white house. The street had taken Sara Sue up, the incline had been unnoticeable until she stopped to look around. She could see Michelle and the person she was meeting better on the hill than she would have been able to if she had stayed on the first street, and for that she was thankful.

Sara Sue hoped it looked like she had been parked there for a while but knew it didn't. Hidden in plain sight was an oxymoron. She was sure Michelle and whoever she was meeting could see her as clearly as she could see them. She hoped they would be too interested in each other to notice her.

Michelle got out of the car and slammed the door. A man got out of the other car and made his way to Michelle's driver side with the speed of a cheetah; it was so fast Sara Sue wasn't sure she saw him take steps so much as glide. He was saying something, spitting the words at Michelle. Sara Sue rolled her windows down, praying the wind would carry their voices to her.

Hand gestures.

Angry postures.

The man leaned into Michelle, seeming to swell up and bear down on her. Michelle held her ground and didn't back away, but she seemed smaller beneath his display of machismo and Sara Sue didn't like it. She didn't like it one bit.

Sara Sue caught words on the air, snippets, phrases.

"What the fuck...?"

"Son of a...!"

Michelle's voice sounded very weak even though she was obviously angry as hell.

"Went down to..."

"Calvin..."

"Lunch with..."

"Not your fucking...!"

"Stupid bitch..."

Both of them dished out as good as they got.

"Calvin?"

Sara Sue couldn't contain the smile spreading across her lips. It was like a movie! Was that the man from the dark-colored car's name? Or was Michelle talking about someone else?

The guy was pretty upset.

Maybe he was Michelle's boyfriend and thought she was fooling around with someone named Calvin. That made sense. Michelle was a pretty girl and the guy losing his mind in front of her was nothing to write home about, at least as far as Michelle could see. Spiky hair and attitude—that's what stood out from where Sara Sue sat, and that wasn't enough. If, by some miracle, he had been able to get Michelle to be his girlfriend, Sara Sue could see why he'd be jealous of every man who gave Michelle a sideways glance.

The two of them seemed to dance as they argued, moving away from Michelle's driver-side door, down the corridor created by the two cars, toward the back of the man's car. The arm flailing and finger pointing didn't stop. It was like watching two birds puff out their feathers in a display of dominance.

Seemingly out of nowhere, Michelle squared her shoulders and raised her hand. The clash of skin against skin as Michelle smacked the man across the face was audible. The slap turned the man's head and buckled his knees; Michelle had come from downtown with that hit. After surveying her handiwork for only a second, she turned to walk away and almost made it to her rear bumper when the man straightened up and lunged at her. He grabbed her arm and yanked her back, making Michelle lose her balance. She fell against his car and, after realizing where she had landed, arched her back and seemed to bounce off the side panel, bringing herself to an upright stance. The man hit Michelle, spinning her head with the force of the blow, knocking her back into the car, but again she righted herself and faced him. Sara Sue felt like she should do something, drive down the street with her lights flashing, blow the horn, call someone... do something. But she was frozen, immobile.

She didn't have time to do anything anyway.

The next hit bent Michelle over the trunk of the man's car and kept her there. He leaned over her, bringing his face close enough to kiss her. Sara Sue couldn't tell if he said something, but he must have. He probably did sneak a kiss in while he was down there too, unable to resist being so close. The look of satisfaction on his face when he stood erect again confirmed it.

Sara Sue wanted to help, wanted to move, but she was stuck. She felt like one of those callous people who hears someone crying for help and turns up their television to drown them out.

The man stood over Michelle a couple seconds longer, looking at what must have been a bloody, damaged face. With the fluidity and grace of a dancer, he strode behind his car, taking care not to bump Michelle as he passed her. He selected a large stone from a piling that marked the end of the parking space and the beginning of the walking path and carried it over to where Michelle now lay on the ground. She had slipped off the trunk, the dead weight of her lower half had been enough to shift the balance and pull her torso off the car. Michelle had crumbled to the ground, arms splayed, legs crossed unnaturally at the shins.

She wasn't moving.

The man stood over her with the stone in his hands.

Michelle must have looked so small and vulnerable.

My God, am I really going to let this happen? Sara Sue thought. Her inaction was answer enough.

In one motion, the man raised the stone above his head, then brought it down onto Michelle's. Over and over again, the stone crashed into Michelle's head. A faint moaning filled the car and it took a while for Sara Sue to recognize the voice as her own. She felt like she was going to faint. She groped for the handle of the glove compartment, searching desperately for the bottled water she usually kept there, not really wanting to drink it, but not wanting to be sick or to pass out either. Her hand landed on something she hadn't expected: a camera.

Karen's camera.

She slid the camera out of the glove compartment, oblivious to the water bottle dislodging, tumbling out of its hiding place and onto the floor of the passenger side.

Sara Sue turned the camera on, careful to hide the glow of the LCD screen beneath the dash. Instinct kicked in and Sara Sue took pictures, zooming in as close as the camera would go before distorting. She could see Michelle's body on the ground, the tangled mess of hair and blood, her legs, bent and dirty, her arms splayed to either side. She looked dead, even from where Sara Sue was sitting.

Michelle, the girl she envied, the girl she wanted to be, was dead on the ground in the parking lot of a closed park.

The man stood over Michelle, looking down at her body with satisfaction mixed with resolution etched on his face. Sara Sue stared at him; his arrogance was so overwhelming that she missed the chance to get a clear shot of his face. Sara Sue was afraid of him even though she was far enough away to speed off if she needed to. She had never knowingly looked at a person who had done such a thing. A murderer. He killed Michelle in cold blood right in front of Sara Sue's eyes. She was looking at a monster.

The man looked around the park once more before he got in his car to leave. Afraid he would see movement, Sara Sue waited until he turned his head to look for oncoming traffic before taking a picture of him. She also got a shot of his license plate before he sped away, leaving Michelle to the elements.

Within minutes the man had pulled into a parking lot, killed Michelle, and driven away. The whole thing had taken as long as stopping for fast food might. Or filling up a gas tank.

Sara Sue waited for what seemed like an hour before she approached the parking lot. She was afraid the man might come back to look at what he had done one more time. But no one came. Not the man, not the police, not even a passerby. The neighborhood was quiet. Michelle and Sara Sue were outside alone.

She got out of her car, leaving it parked where it was; she was afraid to turn the engine over and draw attention to herself. She walked in the shadows, using them to conceal her. She stood beneath the tree at the end of the street for five minutes before finally deciding to cross it and enter the parking lot.

Sara Sue heard the gravel crunch beneath her feet. The sound was reassuring on some levels. She would hear someone if they tried to sneak up on her. But the sound also reminded her that she was awake, that this was not a dream, and that she really was standing there in front of a dead girl.

Sara Sue felt sick.

She had witnessed something she never would have seen if she had just gone home. Instead, she had sat in the car, watched the murder like it was a television show, and then waited until the coast was clear, and for what? To catch a glimpse of the body up close? To gawk at the girl she thought was oh-so-cool as she lay dead on the ground? What did that mean for Sara Sue? What did that mean *about* her?

Michelle's shoe lay on the gravel turned on its side. It must have fallen off when she fell to the ground. There was no blood on it, not like in the movies where every item of clothing the deceased owned had blood on it, providing a clue for the poor sap who stumbled upon the body while out for a jog. It was just a shoe—a regular, nondescript, black leather slide with a low heel. Sara Sue was tempted to pick it up, to touch something of Michelle's, but knew she shouldn't. Her fingerprints didn't need to be anywhere near a dead girl.

Sara Sue let her eyes travel up to Michelle's face, her ruined head. The girl had been pretty. Not beautiful in the traditional Hollywood way, but certainly better looking than most. Her full hair was spread out on the ground, haloing her head. Her mouth was open, the whites of her teeth showing through bloodstained lips. Her left nostril was caked with blood. Her left eye was obliterated, but her right eye was intact. There were broken blood vessels, but they didn't dull the beautiful brown hue of her iris.

The eye seemed to stare at Sara Sue, to mark her.

It was time for Sara Sue to leave and let go. Soon someone would come by and notice Michelle lying there, and they would call the police. The police would take her to the morgue where someone would try to figure out what happened. Then her family would get her body and lay her to rest. Sara Sue hated herself for letting Michelle die, but she wasn't going to be found standing over her because of it.

Sara Sue took a step away but turned back to look at Michelle one last time.

There was one last thing she needed to do.

Sara Sue raised the camera and snapped a picture of Michelle's bloody head.

CHAPTER 5

Sara Sue kept the windows down while she drove home. She didn't need the cool night air to keep her awake—she didn't think she'd ever sleep again, not after what she had seen—she just couldn't bear to be in the closed-up car with the windows shut. It felt too much like a tomb.

Sara Sue couldn't stop thinking about what had just happened. Her thoughts ran together, blurring, distorting, mangling the images, adding things to them, taking other things away.

What kind of car had the man been driving?

What had he been wearing?

Could she describe him—had she even gotten a decent look at his face?

The scene kept running through her mind as Sara Sue doubled back toward the mall, made her usual turn, and left the more populated area—the area dotted with stores and gas stations and signs that lit up the night—to enter the repetitiveness of tract houses, street after street of the same thing, the only difference being their facades: vinyl siding or brick. She had been cultivating a profound hatred for that place, but now it seemed to warm her with its uniformity and calculated din.

People live here.

People she'd seen before, people who would look outside if they heard shouting, people who would have intervened if they had seen what she had just witnessed. People cared about each other in her little part of the world.

Didn't they?

Sara Sue didn't want to think too deeply about it—didn't want to chip away at the armor that calmed her as she sat alone in her car.

She turned into her driveway and sat there with the car idling. She slammed her head into the headrest and stared at the roll bar and the insulated top. She was afraid—of what, she didn't know. Even though she wanted to rid herself of the night, wanted to jump in the shower and wash it off her like so much dirt, she couldn't make herself open the car door.

Her mind started playing tricks on her. The images in her head were violent and bloody, far worse than what she had seen at the park. Sara Sue imagined a man's face, the features vague, belonging to anyone and everyone at the same time, contorting into a mask of anger and hatred. He looked like a demon, the mousse-spiked hair that Sara Sue *could* ascribe to him forming horns on either side of his head. She saw Michelle's head explode from the force of the rock, pieces of flesh flinging through the air and hitting the man's car and the ground around her.

Sara Sue thought she was going to vomit.

She searched wildly for something to focus on, something to bring her back to herself, her car, her driveway, her neighborhood, and take her away from the park, away from Michelle's bloody face. She had kept the radio off during the ride home, leaving her in silence with nothing but her thoughts to torment her. The silence had been deafening and Sara Sue was suddenly sure that the sound of music, the sound of someone else's voice, would calm her down. She turned on the CD player and filled the cabin with Lover.

Baby, I'm crying all inside because you been lyin'. I been here for you but you just brush me aside.

Sara Sue didn't care what Troy was saying. He could have been singing about kicking a girl out in the rain on the side of the highway and it wouldn't have mattered. His voice washed over her, calming her more than she thought it would. Troy was her savior. He was her own personal band man.

She waited until the song was over before she turned off the engine and got out of the car. She smoothed her pants with her hands, still damp with sweat, as she approached the front door. Charlie wasn't home; his side of the driveway was as empty as it was when she left the house. She didn't know if that made her happy or not.

CHAPTER 6

The next morning Sara Sue got up at 7:00 as usual. Charlie had gotten home sometime after she had fallen asleep the night before and she was thankful for that. Sara Sue wouldn't have been able to explain why she kept looking out the window every ten minutes or why she seemed jittery. She wasn't ready to talk about it. She didn't know if she ever would be.

Charlie had left before Sara Sue finished making her coffee. A quick kiss on the cheek and he was out the door. When he'd come into the kitchen that morning, he had sung her praises, telling her he loved what she had done with her hair, but none of that mattered to Sara Sue anymore. She had nodded and smiled thinly, hoping Charlie didn't notice that she was somewhere else. He had picked up on something, though, because the smile he'd been holding fell away from his face like glass shattering on the floor. He'd left quickly and quietly after that, fleeing to a world where he understood the people around him, where the people there still liked him.

She felt bad for Charlie; really, she did. He didn't deserve to be treated so badly, but there wasn't anything she could do about it right then.

Sara Sue couldn't have let herself speak to Charlie. She knew that if she had, if she had so much as asked him how the game went the night before, she would have told him everything—about Michelle and the fact that she had been stalking her for days, about the murder, about the blood. She would have told him and Charlie wouldn't have known how to process it. He would have wanted to go to the police, but they couldn't. He would have wanted to contact someone—Michelle's job, the newspaper, somebody—but that couldn't happen either. What if the man found out and came after her? What if he was just waiting to see what she would do, would leave her alone if she did nothing, but kill her if she told?

A person capable of bashing a pretty girl's head in would probably do anything to save his skin.

The thought gave her chills.

Sara Sue knew that Charlie couldn't help her deal with what she saw and that he'd never be able to keep it a secret either. Who could? She knew it wasn't even fair to ask him to be quiet about something like this. Sara Sue knew *she* shouldn't be quiet about it either—she knew she should tell the police, but a new fear had crept into her head.

Had waiting to report it made her an accessory?

Probably.

Yes, most likely.

She was terrified.

So instead, she had been cold to Charlie and he had left her alone.

She was *alone*.

Now that he was gone, Sara Sue wished he were there, if for no other reason than to protect her when the boogeyman came.

CHAPTER 7

Sara Sue stayed inside all day, nursing paranoia.

Was the killer out there?

Had he seen her drive away?

Did he know who she was?

Ridiculous.

He couldn't have seen her.

He had been long gone by the time she went in for a closer look, and he had been too preoccupied with killing someone to notice a car parked on a hill on another street. But she couldn't shake the feeling that she was being watched, being stalked. She wondered if Michelle had sensed anything weird over the past couple days when Sara Sue had been the one doing the stalking; if the hair on the back of her neck had stood at attention the way Sara Sue's did now.

After wasting all day looking over her shoulder, as she lay in bed staring at the ceiling that night, Sara Sue realized that she *had* to go outside. She had forgotten something. Something important. A little voice in her head chastised her for it, reminded her who she was—just a boring old housewife who wasn't cut out for things like this. And considering the size of the mistake, she was inclined to believe it. Still, none of that changed the fact that she had to get up out of bed and do something about it.

She had to go outside.

She waited until Charlie was asleep to do it—she didn't want him to see the camera.

When she opened the front door, the car seemed so far away.

She tried to relax a little as she walked to the car. *He never saw me*, she told herself. *He didn't*. She had been too far away and he had too much on his mind to worry about her parked car at the top of the hill a street over. She hadn't done anything to draw attention to herself and she had waited long enough after he left to be sure he was really gone before moving a muscle.

Famous last words.

As Sara Sue opened the car door, she contemplated going to the police for the umpteenth time. She went through the pros and cons, trying to get her thoughts together. They might ask her why she waited so long to report the murder; they might think she had something to do with it. How would she explain following Michelle in the first place? How lame does it sound to say that she saw this girl in the mall, thought she was hot and she wanted to be like her, and so she had followed her to see what her life was like? They'd think that she, the guy, and Michelle were part of some love triangle. How the hell could she get herself out of *that*?

Sara Sue couldn't say anything. To anyone. Charlie wouldn't understand either. He would think she had followed the girl because she wanted to *be with* her instead of just *be* her because sex was always the answer for him. Karen just wouldn't get it at all; the whole fantasizing-emulating thing would be over her head. Sara Sue didn't even understand it anymore now that she was seeing it from the outside looking in.

It was over—the fantasy she had been weaving for herself.

It had to be.

Things were too dangerous for it not to be.

Sara Sue grabbed the camera—at least she'd had the good sense to put it back in the glove compartment at some point during the whole ordeal instead of leaving it on the seat, visible to anyone who cared to look, the way she feared she had—and got out of the car. She didn't want to look at the pictures, wanted no part of them anymore, but she had one last thing to do with them before it could really be over. She was too afraid to do it in the dark of night; her imagination didn't need any more fodder than it already had.

In the morning, she told herself.

It'll all be over in the morning.

CHAPTER 8

There were newspapers still on the table when she came into the kitchen early the next morning. Charlie was still asleep.

Charlie had brought them in when he came home from work the night before, but Sara Sue had avoided them; she'd left them sitting there through dinner, pushed to the far side of the table as they ate in virtual silence. She hadn't wanted to read anything about Michelle, hadn't wanted to rehash any of the gory details of the night before. But there they were, sitting on the kitchen table, waiting to be read. If they were still sitting there when he came home from work and added more to the stack, Charlie would find it odd—reading the newspaper every day was one of her *things*. She could just throw them out, but she wouldn't. Even though she didn't want to relive what happened, a part of her just had to know what the news was saying about it. Morbid curiosity at its finest.

She disgusted herself.

Sara Sue sat down, the morning sun just beginning to peak out over the horizon. It was early—much earlier than her usual time up, but she wasn't surprised. That she had been able to fall asleep in the first place is what blew her mind. She stifled a yawn that rose up to punctuate the sentiment. Sara Sue opened the local paper first, pushing aside the national one for later. If there was anything about Michelle out there, it was more than likely in the local paper.

Nothing on the front page. She had not expected there to be. The murder hadn't happened in the same town where Sara Sue lived—it had been in the same county, but a few towns over—so although she expected there to be coverage, the story would probably be buried deeper in. But then Sara Sue remembered the way Michele's face looked and thought differently. Nothing like that had happened in their area in, like, ever. That alone might rate front page coverage—maybe even for more than one day.

As she flipped through, Sara Sue found a story about a local politician she secretly wished would keel over, a story about an old lady and her dog winning a pet and owner contest held at the mall, some commentary on the state of the war, and other pieces of small-paper junk.

Nothing about Michelle.

She pushed back from the table and sighed. Why wasn't there anything about Michelle's murder? You would think with gore like that the news would mention *something*. It wasn't every day that someone got murdered out there in the burbs, let alone like that. The town Michelle died in wasn't as nice as Sara Sue's little slice of suburban heaven, but it was still relatively quiet. It wasn't like living in the inner city—not by a long shot.

So where was it?

Sara Sue dropped the newspaper and drummed her fingers on the table. She looked at the camera she had brought in from the car and tapped some more. Nothing in the newspaper, nothing on the radio, at least not yet. What if there's nothing on the camera? What if she had imagined the whole thing?

The prospect made Sara Sue happy and nervous at the same time. Happy because if it was all in her head, if it was all some crazy nightmare that started and ended with her being loco, then that was fine. At least it would be over and Michelle wouldn't be dead. At least she wouldn't have let someone be killed while she watched. It made her nervous too; if all of this was in Sara Sue's head, what the hell was wrong with her?

Sara Sue looked at the camera, afraid of it now.

Sighing, she got up from the table and walked into the living room. She turned on the television. Maybe there would be something on the tube about what happened.

First there was a promo for the main newscast in the morning, coverage about everything happening in the world. But it was the local news she was interested in. Local news liked to run a murder into the ground—you just had to watch any local television station for a few days and that fact would become undeniably clear. And if you're near a major city like New York or DC, stories about murders are the *only* stories you'll see for the hour-long broadcast. Sara Sue thought that maybe they'd mention that they've apprehended a suspect in the "community park murder"—how was that for a title? Then this whole thing would be over and she could put it to bed. But would she? Or would she follow the case, waiting to see what would happen to the guy with the spiked hair? Would she go to the courthouse and listen to testimony just so she could hear all the sordid details that made up Michelle's life? Sara Sue didn't know, and that scared her.

Later, she woke up on the sofa to sunlight in her eyes, the smell of coffee filling her nostrils, and the sound of the most sickening-sweet voice she had ever heard—Arielle, the weather girl. When her eyes finally adjusted, she saw Charlie sitting at the table reading the newspaper she'd left open. His coffee mug had already been filled and she could see the steam coming off the top. His head was bent, his eyes engrossed; he was probably reading the sports page. His right hand drummed the table much as hers had earlier. His fingers were dangerously close to the camera.

Sara Sue stood up really fast and tried to make a spectacle of it, stretching and yawning loudly, hoping he would hear her and turn around.

It worked.

"Hey babe. I tried to be quiet so I didn't wake you."

Sometimes she loved her sweet old boy… but now was not the time to show it.

"Hi, Charlie," she said flatly.

"What were you doing out here?" Charlie asked, further endearing himself to her. "Did my snoring bother you?"

"Yeah, it did," Sara Sue said, wishing she hadn't had to lie like that. "You know, you really ought to look into that. You stop breathing sometimes."

He didn't, but hell, it sounded good.

"I do? It doesn't feel like it." Poor Charlie, genuinely perplexed.

"Just because you don't feel it doesn't mean it isn't happening. People who get their heads chopped off don't feel it either, but that doesn't mean it didn't happen."

Where the hell had that come from? Sara Sue wondered. From the look on Charlie's face, he was wondering the same thing.

"Well, I'll see about it. I'll mention it to the doc the next time I go."

"Yeah, you do that," Sara Sue said with as much disdain as she could. She needed Charlie to leave, just get up and go to work. The camera was sitting at the edge of the table, close enough for Charlie to knock it over. Even though there was lots of other stuff on the table, too—books she had been meaning to read, a stack of coasters, things she had forgotten about as soon as she had set them down—he would notice the camera after a while, realize it wasn't theirs. She was surprised he hadn't already.

She couldn't let him see the pictures.

Sara Sue made her way over to the sink, thinking, thinking.

But instead of leaving, Charlie took a sip of coffee and turned his attention back to the newspaper. Sara Sue looked between the top of his head and the camera, panic creeping up the back of her neck. He was settled in, enjoying his coffee and he had quite a bit of it left. He wouldn't be leaving any time soon.

She had to think of something.

"Hey, what's the camera doing up here?" Charlie said over the top of the newspaper.

Panic flashed on Sara Sue's face. She reached for the knob, turned on the water, did all of it too fast. She hoped Charlie didn't notice.

"What do you think it's up here for?" The shrillness of her voice caught her off guard as much as it did Charlie. "What do you think, I'm taking naked pictures of myself and posting them on the Internet?"

What a deep-end comment. Sara Sue hoped that would be enough to throw him off her trail, make him think she had woken up on the wrong side of the bed and was being a bitch this morning. Again.

"Well, yeah, maybe."

The look of concern on his face made Sara Sue sad.

She put on the most disgusted face she could muster and hissed, "Jesus, Charlie. Get a life."

That did it. Charlie shook his head and looked back down at the paper. Within seconds he was taking a last gulp from his mug, getting up, and making his way to the front door.

"It's Karen's camera," Sara Sue said, her tone a little gentler, the bite gone. She felt bad about what just happened. She didn't want him leaving pissed off at her. Things were bad enough between them as it was.

Sara Sue walked toward the bedroom, camera in hand.

"She left it in the car and I brought it in. I didn't want anybody to see it in the window and steal it."

Charlie hesitated, weighing his words. Finally, he muttered a muted, "Okay," but she could see that things were definitely not okay.

"We took pictures of her for one of those online dating sites. She had me all over the place looking for backdrops."

Charlie's face was blank. He didn't believe a word she was saying.

A cold silence sat between them. Sara Sue looked away.

"Well, I'll be late tonight," Charlie finally said. "We're going to Gordon's."

"Another night at the bar, huh? You're turning into a lush."

"We're just shooting pool, Sara Sue. I never have more than two beers the whole time," Charlie said, his voice still measured. It bothered Sara Sue more than she thought it would.

"Whatever," she said, making it into the bedroom and managing to look like she had better things to do than talk to him.

Charlie sighed, said goodbye over his shoulder, and then he was gone.

Sara Sue waited until she heard the front door lock before letting out the breath she had been holding. But she wasn't safe yet. She had to move. Charlie could come back and demand to see just what the hell was on the camera that had gotten her dander up so high in the first place. Karen would probably be calling any minute asking for her camera back. There was no time to waste.

Sara Sue sat on the bed and held the camera in her lap. It felt like a rock sitting there—heavy, unyielding. She touched it, played with the zoom wheel, touched the frame of the lens, but she didn't turn it on. What if there was nothing but Karen's headshots on there?

Accomplice to murder or lunatic... neither option would make it all better—make it like it was.

After sitting there for what seemed like an hour, Sara Sue turned the camera on and changed the mode to view, all with her eyes squeezed shut. The last picture she had taken was sitting on the LCD screen just waiting for her to look at it. Her face was starting to burn, like the image itself was boring into her. Sara Sue had to look now—there was no turning back.

She opened her eyes to a squint, barely able to make out anything except that whatever was on the LCD screen was dark.

Not good enough.

She opened her eyes slowly, letting the image come into view in stages.

There she was.

Michelle's bloodied face filled the LCD screen. All the emotions came rushing back—how frightened she had been sitting out there in the dark, how sad she was for Michelle having to die like that, how disappointed she was in herself for not doing anything to stop it. Another thought crept into her mind—one she wasn't proud of: relief that she wasn't crazy.

Okay, so the hard part's over. What now?

An idea flashed in her mind. Something she could do to make it right, or try to, anyway.

Sara Sue tore her eyes away from the image of Michelle's head and forced herself to look at the other pictures. She was looking for something she could use—something that would help her do what needed to be done. She had only taken four pictures the whole time she was out there. One of them was too dark to see anything in; one was a profile of the man, but it was really hard to make out his features; one was of Michelle's head, which came out clearer than she wished it had; and the other was of the license plate. The iridescent paint they used on the plate made it come up clear as day. A smile played at the corners of Sara Sue's lips as she looked at the picture of the license plate.

Are you really gonna do this? she thought. *This is real life, not some silly game you're playing with yourself.*

And that was true, but real life was boring Sara Sue to tears. At least this would spice things up a bit. And she could do right by a girl who deserved better than she got.

Sara Sue took the memory card out of Karen's camera and put

it in her photo printer. She loaded the printer with glossy paper and printed the last four photos from the camera.

I'm going to do this. For Michelle. And for me, she vowed. *I just have to figure out how.*

CHAPTER 9

Sara Sue left the house soon after printing the pictures. She deleted them from Karen's camera while sitting in the car leaving herself only the printed images; now they weren't saved anywhere. She started down the street, driving like a bat out of hell, then jerked her foot off the pedal like a teenager learning to drive a stick shift for the first time. She had to keep calm, act normal. She couldn't draw attention to herself, and speeding through the neighborhood wasn't exactly going to keep her incognito. The last thing she needed right now was to get pulled over with those pictures in her purse.

Sara Sue started again, driving moderately, just under the speed limit. She felt like she was crawling but that's where she kept it the rest of the way out of her community. She picked up the pace substantially once she hit the straight-away and headed toward the park where Michelle had been killed. She retraced her steps to the park, keeping her speed natural, trying not to look like she was looking for something. Along the way, she noticed a library—a small, one-floor stone building standing alone on a

street populated with a mix of residential and commercial proper-
ties. If the building housed a thousand books, she'd be surprised. It
was the size of a small house, the kind her grandmother had lived
in all of her life. Little and cramped but she called it cozy. Falls
Junction Library, the sign read. Sara Sue pulled into the lot and
parked.

Falls Junction.

So that's where she was.

Nice enough name but one Sara Sue never wanted to hear
again after this was all over.

She sat in the car, her legs feeling heavy. She had to go inside
because it only made sense. A library might have a community
newspaper—in fact, the library, the gas station, and supermarket
were the only places she could think of that might have a supply of
them at the front of the building so she could grab one and go. If
they did, maybe there would be something in it about Michelle.

She sighed, squeezed her eyes shut.

Opened her eyes and looked back at the building.

This is it, Sara Sue thought. *If you get out of the car, you've
committed to this.*

She hesitated a second longer and then pulled the door handle.

You wanted to shake things up. Well, here goes nothing.

The stand for the *Falls Junction Tribune* was positioned on the
wall along with a children's storytelling class schedule, library
tutorial signup sheets, and a missing person's poster. Sara Sue
walked casually over to the stand, looked at the flyers on the wall
for a second, then picked up a newspaper and left the library.

She realized she'd been holding her breath when she got back
to the car. She couldn't stop herself from smiling as she got in, as
grotesque as the notion seemed to her subconscious—the part of
her not 100 percent interested in playing the game. This was
exactly the kind of pick-me-up her life needed: a secret mission.
Her excitement only waned a little when she thought about the
picture of Michelle in her purse.

"I'm gonna do this," Sara Sue said aloud in the privacy of her car, "I'm going to find Michelle's killer."

CHAPTER 10

Just *how* she planned to do that was another story altogether.

After leaving the library, Sara Sue turned onto a side street that looked like all the other ones around it—bungalows placed too close to each other, sharing the cracked sidewalk that lined the street. She parked behind a covered jalopy and opened the *Falls Junction Tribune.* She hit pay dirt almost immediately. The article was on the second page.

WOMAN FOUND MURDERED IN JOPLIN PARK IDENTIFIED

Sara Sue sat back in her seat as she started to read, hoping she looked like everybody else.

Wait.

No one else was parked on the side of the street reading the newspaper. Most people take their newspapers into their houses and read them or go somewhere and read them over a cup of coffee. Most people don't sit in their car on a warm day, parked in front of somebody's house, and just... read.

No.

Right then Sara Sue wasn't blending in. She was sticking out like a sore thumb.

Sara Sue started the car and Lover blasted through her speakers. She turned it down fast and craned her head around, looking to see if anyone noticed her. People in neighborhoods like this knew everyone on their street and recognized the cars of the people who came to visit them regularly. They would remember a stranger. Especially one in a convertible blasting dated music in the morning.

Sara Sue gripped the steering wheel tightly as she turned around. She noticed that the curtains were closed in most of the windows of the houses lining the street; maybe everyone was at work. Still, she wanted to get off that street. No sense tempting fate. Sara Sue made a right onto the street the library was on and headed back in the direction of the mall.

Sara Sue felt like she'd already made a couple mistakes but felt sure nobody had noticed. The librarian was too busy reading *Us* magazine when she'd snagged the newspaper, and maybe luck had been in her favor and the people who lived on that side street were all at work instead of sitting at home, looking out of the window or running around town like she was, acting like Columbo, getting home just in time to see a suspicious car with a suspicious woman inside, behaving... well... suspiciously.

Now all she needed to do was get out of Falls Junction without leaving a trace.

CHAPTER 11

Sara Sue drove to more familiar surroundings—the mall. She figured she'd go to Starbucks and read the paper. That's what people do at coffee shops and bookstore cafes: work on their laptops, read books and newspapers, look studious. Sara Sue could pull that off.

She bought a brownie and sat down at one of those ridiculously small, but trendy little tables and opened the paper. She was about to start reading when she realized she was holding the paper up, showing the page to anyone who glanced over to look. She lowered the newspaper a bit, trying to look natural as she did it, fighting the urge to snatch it out of view and make a ruckus that people would crane their necks to identify, maybe even give the side eye about. She settled into her chair, took a deep breath, took a bite of her brownie, and started to read.

"The body found at Joplin Park on Tuesday morning has been identified as that of Falls Junction resident Christina Tally. Tally, a 23-year-old retail worker and lifetime resident of Falls Junction, was found brutally beaten and left in the parking lot of

Joplin Park. Police say there is no evidence that Tally was sexually assaulted.

The Tally family says Christina didn't have any enemies; however, she moved away from the family home two years ago. Coworkers say she left work in good spirits on Tuesday night and spoke of going home to relax. Ms. Tally never made it home.

Police are investigating several leads and expect to speak with her b—"

"Terrible, isn't it?"

Sara Sue jumped. It was as if the girl was yelling in her ear. A young woman, probably the same age as Michelle, was standing over Sara Sue, shaking her head.

"I can't believe something like that happened around here," the girl continued. "Yeah," Sara Sue said, noncommittally.

"I know that girl, too. She worked right here in the mall and she's, like, always here. It's kinda like her second home, know what I mean? I've shopped in the store she worked in before, too, but it isn't really one of my favorites because they charge too much for a pair of jeans, know what I mean? Money is tight and I can't just throw it away on some crap I can get for less somewhere else. Anyway, I know I've seen her before, I just can't believe—."

Sara Sue felt like she was going deaf. The girl's voice was high-pitched and she was talking a mile a minute without an end in sight. It took everything Sara Sue had not to tell the girl to shut her freaking mouth and move on.

"I mean, I can almost *see* Joplin Park from my window," the girl continued.

She hadn't taken a breath yet.

"Nobody knows if the guy, like, knew her or something, and followed her or if it was just random. But, like, why would she have stopped at the park at night? It's closed and everybody knows that. So, he probably wasn't just hanging around waiting for somebody to, like, pass by or something. So, the guy *had* to know her, know what I mean?"

Sara Sue had barely shown that she was giving the woman approval to go on, but that didn't matter. It didn't seem like the woman was really looking at her anyway—she could have been talking to anyone right then.

"He knew her and they met at the park or he followed her and forced her to pull over or something. I've lived there forever. I pretty much know everyone around there. What if I know the guy who did it? Oh my God, it could be anyone! God! Doesn't that just freak you out?"

Sara Sue had been nodding while she was talking, at first just to placate her, but then to keep her going. She was telling Sara Sue things she needed to know in her babble, and as hard as it was to sit there and listen to her grating voice, she needed to hear what the girl had to say.

"Yeah, it's scary," Sara Sue said, hoping she'd start back up.

"Like, nobody's safe. Nobody. You gotta be careful all the time now. That is so scary. My friend Jen says there's a tribute page out there for her on MySpace. She thinks the killer is probably going onto the site and, like, checking out what people are saying about her. Like it gets him off or something. I was gonna go on there and see for myself, but I don't know. I guess it kind of creeps me out."

"I bet."

The girl nodded. Either she was just resting before she started up again or she was finished.

Sara Sue waited, not breathing.

Three seconds.

More.

The girl was done.

Sara Sue folded up the newspaper and stood up. She wasn't done—she'd only had a bite of her brownie and hadn't touched her drink, but she couldn't risk someone coming up behind her again. She had almost spit up the first time. She couldn't let that happen again.

"It's terrible," Sara Sue said and realized she shouldn't be talking so much. What if someone remembered the woman who was reading about the murder in the newspaper while she munched gleefully on a brownie? She hadn't been smiling or anything like that, hadn't done anything that someone might actually call *gleeful*, but you never knew what people might say when questions start getting asked.

She was getting paranoid.

She couldn't help it.

"Yeah, well, I guess I talked your ear off," the girl said. "This whole thing just has me kind of, I don't know, freaked out, I guess."

"It has all of us freaked out," Sara Sue said wishing could just stay silent instead but knowing that would have seemed weird. She lowered her voice, put on her best reassuring tone. "Just try to stay safe."

"Yeah, that's all we can do, right?"

Sara Sue nodded and started to walk away, hoping the girl didn't ask where she lived in Falls Junction. After all, if she didn't live there, why would she be reading their newspaper?

She picked up her pace, hoping the girl didn't ask her anything at all.

"Well, you be safe, too," the girl said.

Sara Sue smiled, threw out the brownie and drink, and merged into the mall foot traffic.

CHAPTER 12

Sara Sue wanted to get in the car, go home, lock the door, and hide in her bedroom, but she knew she couldn't. If anyone was watching her, it would seem weird that she'd go all the way to the mall to get brownie at Starbucks—especially when there was practically a Starbucks on every street corner–and then not even finish it. She made herself walk around the mall, hoping she didn't look as aimless as she was. Before she realized where she was going, she was standing in front of that trendy little clothing store she had been in the other day. The store where Michelle had worked.

Should she go in? Would the other girl who was working that day remember her? Why would she? Sara Sue was just another customer, right? Just someone who browsed the racks, bought a little something, and left. What's to remember about somebody like that? Nothing, right?

Sara Sue felt uneasy as she walked into the store, but she couldn't stop herself. Morbid curiosity had reared its ugly head again. She wanted to see how people behaved now that Michelle had been identified. Was the store busier than usual? Were people talking about her openly in the aisles, chatting about the dead girl that used to work there as they picked through the clothes on the racks?

Sara Sue felt like a voyeur… and it was exciting.

On some disturbing level, the whole thing was exciting—being in Michelle's store, driving around her town, doing the detective work.

There has to be some kind of syndrome for this—some kind of problem on the books, because this doesn't seem normal, she thought, but that didn't stop her.

She might need therapy when this was all over.

Sara Sue went over to one of the racks that had pants that didn't look big enough to tug up past her knees and tried to look as if she was really interested in them. The store *was* pretty busy, curiosity making women fill the aisles. Everybody was kind of looking around at the walls and at each other, uncertain what to do but wanting to be right where they were. The clothes were secondary. Sara Sue didn't know if she should join in or actually shop.

She was just about to walk out when a girl came up to her the same way Michelle had a couple days ago.

"Are you finding everything okay?"

She had to clear her throat to answer. The girl was wearing a button with Michelle's face on it, smiling and prettily. It was a homemade button with a black and white picture that had likely been a printed out copy of her employee ID, but it was still flattering; it really showed the contours of her face—Sara Sue thought, not for the first time, that Michelle could have modeled if she wanted to.

"No, no, I'm fine, thanks," Sara Sue stammered.

"Okay. Well, I'm Kerri. Let me know if you need anything."

When Kerri walked over to help someone else Sara Sue left the store.

CHAPTER 13

After she left the store, Sara Sue headed to her car, deciding that she really needed to kick it up a notch. That poor girl—Christina, Sara Sue reminded herself, because she might as well start calling her by the right name since the fantasy was over—was dead. She was dead because some bastard caved her head in. Sara Sue saw him do it, which made her part of the whole thing. She had to do something for that woman. For *Tina*, her subconscious voiced, giving the woman she would never know a nickname.

Tina.

She had to do something for Tina—better late than never.

She drove to a McDonald's parking lot about two miles away from the mall, parked, and finished reading the article.

"Police are investigating several leads and expect to speak with her boyfriend, who attends college in Washington, DC. His whereabouts have been confirmed on the night of Tally's murder and he is not considered a person of interest.

A private wake will proceed the funeral on Wednesday, September 24th at Proctor Funeral Home. The family has asked

that, in lieu of flowers, donations be made to Allison's Table in Christina Tally's name."

So, the boyfriend was in college in DC. That wasn't very far away—about an hour and a half without traffic. So, if he drove there after Tina got off work, followed her to the park, killed her, and high-tailed it back to school, he would have been back on campus in time to hit the first party and no one would have been suspicious. He could have had a beer in hand by 11:30.

Is that what happened?

Sara Sue could feel her adrenaline starting to flow. This was a real lead.

But what if the boyfriend didn't do it? What if he was on campus with his friends the whole time and nowhere near Falls Junction? What if he told his boys he was coming out to see his girlfriend and he really went to hang out with some chick from another school? What if everybody knew he was going to be with that girl and it was no secret he was cheating? Long distance relationships hardly ever work. Maybe Tina had somebody on the side too. Maybe that guy on the side was the one who killed her.

Sara Sue laid her head on the headrest and closed her eyes.

This is real, she thought again. It was a real murder with a real victim. What did she think she was doing? Was she really going to hunt the guy down? *Could* she?

Sara Sue opened her eyes and watched a kid go into McDonald's with his mother. A man holding a bag in one hand and French fries in the other held the door open for them with his elbow. She watched life pass her by as she sat in her car. Just like she had the night Tina was killed.

Sara Sue turned the key in the ignition. She *was* going after that murdering bastard.

Better late than never.

CHAPTER 14

Charlie came home midday to find the house empty. He wasn't really all that surprised given the way Sara Sue had been acting. Lately everything he did was wrong, every facial expression he made was perceived as nasty... or stupid. He thought Sara Sue even hated the way he breathed. It would make sense if she was seeing another man—that guy must be everything he wasn't. Tall, dark, handsome—it sounded cliché, but that was what Sara Sue always seemed to like in high school. It made him wonder why she even took a second look at him. The guy was probably smart. Charlie was no slouch, but the guy must be that doctor kind of smart. The way Sara Sue hinted around calling Charlie stupid, he wouldn't be surprised if the guy was a Rhodes Scholar.

That's why he came home. He needed to know what or who he was dealing with. Because something was going on, that was for sure.

Everything used to be fine between the two of them; at least that was what Charlie thought. Sara Sue didn't have to work; they had a nice house in a nice neighborhood. At one time he had hoped to have kids with her, but now he wasn't so sure she wanted to. She was moody, downright mean. She hardly ever looked at him with kindness in her eyes and sex felt more like an obligation than desire. He knew Sara Sue felt the same way. He could see it in her face—that bored expression she adopted, the way she stared at something on the ceiling that was so much more interesting than looking at him. He hated what they had become.

For a long time, Charlie thought it was something about him that was causing their problems, something he was doing that she didn't like. But the way she acted about the camera this morning made him think otherwise. Maybe Sara Sue *did* use Karen's camera to take naked pictures of herself to send to some guy, or maybe the pictures on the camera were of the bastard himself. Or maybe the camera belonged to the guy and he let her take it home to look at their dirty little pictures. Maybe the camera took video also and she was watching their little sexcapade on the LCD screen over and over and over again.

He needed to find that camera.

Charlie looked in the obvious place first—the bedroom. Charlie wondered, as he looked through her dresser drawers, if Sara Sue thought he bought her cockamamie story. Anybody would have seen through it and the anger she displayed; Sara Sue was an open book when it came to lying. She could never do it well, which was one of the things that made him comfortable with her. Charlie always thought he'd know when Sara Sue was lying to him, so he'd had no problem trusting the popular cheerleader who was getting more than her fair share of attention but for some reason had chosen to be with him. He wasn't hard on the eyes, but there were better-looking guys out there who were more her type. But Charlie had never worried about it because he could see right through his sweet Sara Sue. She had never given him a reason to think otherwise.

Until now.

Sara Sue was lying and it was written all over her face. Her stunningly beautiful face. Charlie still loved her even though she had been as mean as a rattlesnake lately. He wanted his marriage to work. They just had to get through the storm they were in and get back on track. That is, if Charlie could stomach what she was hiding.

He didn't find anything in any of the drawers or in the closet. She must have taken the camera with her. Charlie sat down on the bed, some of the wind taken out of his sails. He was starting to second guess himself. Maybe the camera really *was* Karen's and there was nothing lewd on it. Maybe he was blowing things out of proportion, looking for something wrong, some issue he could point to, when the real problem was that Sara Sue just didn't want him anymore.

Charlie sighed and covered his eyes with his hand. He didn't want to believe she was done with him. They had something real; at least they used to. Something had changed; he could admit that, but he didn't know what. All he knew was that he had blown things out of proportion and he was ashamed of himself. Even though Sara Sue was acting odd, even though she seemed to hate him, he should have thought better of her than this.

All he wanted to do now was get out of the house before Sara Sue found him snooping around. What would he say if she caught him there in the middle of the day? He couldn't admit that he was checking up on her, not unless he wanted a divorce.

Charlie looked around, making sure he hadn't dropped anything on the floor that would give him away. He skimmed the bed, the floor near the bed, the desk—the computer monitor light was on. He smiled, suppressing a laugh. If he got a penny for every time he told Sara Sue to turn off the monitor after she was finished with the computer, they would be rich. He let the smile spread across his face as he thought of Sara Sue, the way she was before, way back when they were still in love—her silly smile, her playful wink. He promised himself that he was going to talk to Sara Sue and together they would work their way back to what they used to be.

CHAPTER 15

Sara Sue saw Charlie's car before she turned into the driveway.

What was he doing home?

Her instinct was to run—to go somewhere, anywhere, and wait him out. But she couldn't do that. Paranoia set in again, flushing her skin as she thought of all the ways this could go wrong. People might have seen her drive up. They would think it strange if she drove away knowing her husband was inside. The stay-at-home mom across the street was probably thinking she and Charlie were having a midday rendezvous. Ms. Jenkins, who lived next door, probably thought Charlie was a cheating skunk and that Sara Sue was about to catch him in the act. Sara Sue imagined that both of them damn near had popcorn popped, waiting to see what her face looked like when she got out of the car. Would she be happy or upset? The way she played it would determine what rumors were spread.

Sara Sue didn't need any bad press right now.

She put on her sneakiest, most lascivious smile, and got out of the car—midday rendezvous for those who were keeping score. As she walked up the driveway, an appropriate skip to her step for the lookie-loos, her head was reeling, worrying about what Charlie might have found. Had she left anything out on the bed or on the floor? She had Karen's camera with her; it was still in the glove compartment, so he couldn't be looking at that. Besides, the pictures were already erased. Sara Sue thought she covered all her bases, but still, she worried that Charlie was seeing something he shouldn't be.

She burst into the bedroom faster than she meant to and when she spoke, her voice was loud, like a television with the volume turned way too high.

"Charlie! What are you doing?"

CHAPTER 16

Charlie stopped, his finger hovering over the on/off button on the monitor. So, what's this now? Sara Sue looked guilty of something. Of what, he didn't know, but there was something going on. Sara Sue might think he was a fool, but he wasn't. He had to play this the right way if he was going to find out what was going on, and in that instant, he decided he *did* want to know. Loving someone is one thing, but letting them play you is another. All that talk of trust and nostalgia went out the window, or at least back up on the shelf for now.

"Hey babe," Charlie started off, trying to sound normal, "You left the monitor on again and I was just about to turn it off."

Charlie moved his hand from the on/off button to the mouse instead, though, just to see what Sara Sue would do. She almost jumped out of her skin before regaining control of herself. What the hell was on the computer that Sara Sue didn't want Charlie to see? Chat transcripts? Nude pictures? What?

Charlie was getting mad. It was getting harder and harder to play this game with his mind jumping from one conclusion to the next.

Charlie shook the mouse, waiting to see if the desktop would pop back into view, but it didn't; the CPU was off. He couldn't think of a way to turn it back on without being obvious about it, so he pushed the on/off button on the monitor and let it be. For now.

He didn't say anything, let the silence hang between them. His mother used to tell him to be quiet sometimes and listen. She said that people would talk *for* you to fill in the empty space. And sure enough...

"So, what are you doing home?"

The tone of Sara Sue's voice was softer than it had been in weeks. What should he say? He couldn't tell her he came home to see what she was doing, couldn't say he forgot anything because she would see right through that.

He was taking too long to answer.

"I came home to see what you were doing. I feel like we haven't spent a whole lot of time together recently and I, well I guess I missed you."

If she had laughed out loud, he wouldn't have been surprised. What kind of syrupy, cheesecake sort of reply was that? But it was out there now—too late to pull it back. As Charlie sat back, waiting to take her tongue-lashing, he was dismayed by how much truth he had just revealed.

"Really?"

Sara Sue cocked her head to the side and looked at Charlie in a way she hadn't in a long time.

It felt good to be on the receiving end of that look again. Charlie only hoped Sara Sue wasn't giving that look to anyone else.

CHAPTER 17

Sara Sue hoped it was working.

Charlie was too damned close to the computer.

He still hadn't moved away from the monitor and he looked like he might turn the computer on any second. He wouldn't see anything if he turned the computer on; nothing had been saved on the hard drive or on a CD. But what about the temporary files? What if the computer had saved the images in one of those folders that was labeled in all consonants and buried on the computer in some registry folder, somewhere so deep that they couldn't be found easily? Well, if that were the case, that meant Charlie wouldn't find the pictures any sooner than she would. That should have made her feel better but it didn't. The fear of being caught was irrational but unstoppable. She'd heard people say that nothing is ever truly erased from a computer. If that was really true...

"Really?" she said, hoping that was the right reaction because she had stopped listening to what Charlie was saying about halfway in. It must have been because he softened a bit, looked at her a little longer, expectantly.

Good.

She could still stop Charlie in his tracks. The thought excited her. She actually wanted to have sex with him right then and there —entirely out of the blue. Something about the way he looked— boyish, almost the same as he did in high school. Uninhibited. Young. Eager. Gosh, how had he rolled all those looks into one and tacked on some grown-up sensuality? She didn't know why, but Charlie was really looking good to her right then—better than he had in a long time.

"Yeah, I guess I did." Charlie looked away as he spoke, too shy to meet her eyes.

"So," she said, letting her voice drop and float on the air the way he liked it, breathy and deep. Sara Sue walked toward the bed slowly, saying nothing, keeping eye contact. She could almost feel the heat coming off Charlie's body. Or was it coming from her?

She put her knee on the bed and said, "What do you want to do about it?"

Charlie let his hand fall away from the computer slowly. She noticed it and was happy, but she was more interested in what he planned to do with it next.

CHAPTER 18

The sex was good. Like one of their best, at least in the past couple years. Sara Sue just let go. She felt everything Charlie was doing, and boy, was he doing some nice things. She let herself see him, really see his body for what it was and not what her mind had made him out to be. She hadn't realized she had been imagining him as someone unappealing, had been attributing body flaws to him that were not there. No, he didn't have his high-school-football-star body anymore, but she didn't have her cheerleader body either. She could stand to lose a few pounds around the middle just like most people her age. So why was she making Charlie out to be some disgusting pig? His legs were still as strong and as beautiful as ever, his midsection was soft but not jiggling, his arms were tight... what the hell had she been looking at?

It was like they shook off the people they had been for the past couple of months and donned their old selves. They touched each other better. They *wanted* to touch each other, and that made a huge difference. Sara Sue had forgotten how nice it could be.

She almost forgot that she needed to wipe the computer when Charlie left.

CHAPTER 19

Okay, something was definitely up. The sex was just too good for everything to be normal. For months Sara Sue had been treating Charlie like a piece of crap, talking to him like he was bothering her, laying there like a lump on a log the few times they actually had sex, hardly acknowledging him at all except to frown at him. Why today, when she had looked like a deer caught in the headlights in the morning and guilty just now, would she have a change of heart and have sex with him the way she used to? It didn't make sense......unless she had something to hide.

Charlie felt Sara Sue's head pressing into his chest as they lay in bed and wanted to cry. It felt so good, but it was a lie. She was cheating on him. She had to be. The love of his life was messing around. He wanted to confront her right then, demand to know who the guy was, then go and beat the crap out of him, but he couldn't. Not yet. He didn't have any evidence, nothing tangible, and Sara Sue would dismiss anything that wasn't concrete. And then they would be in an even worse spot.

Charlie had to find out what was going on and he had to do it soon. He didn't know how much longer he could act like the idiot Sara Sue thought he was.

CHAPTER 20

Sara Sue needed to get up and get going—she still had a bunch of things to do before Charlie got home from work for the night. Or was he staying home? If he stayed home, she couldn't go back out. She wasn't stupid enough to think their little romp in the sack was enough to placate Charlie for good. He was still at least a little suspicious and she couldn't blame him. She would be too. Sure, she would have already asked him if he was fooling around, but that's just one of the differences between them. She was more straightforward and to the point. Charlie beat around the bush. That used to annoy her, but today it was working in her favor.

Except he wasn't being his usual self, was he? He was home, not at work. The old Charlie would have wondered and brooded over this at work all day long, would have stared at her across the dinner table with a question on his face—one she would have let hang between them had he voiced it and not demanded an answer, demanded discussion. Then he would have gone to bed worrying about what she was doing in the front room. Was she on the phone with her boyfriend, whispering about their next meeting? Or worse yet, were they laughing about Charlie? Was she fantasizing about the other guy in the front room, maybe even doing something about it while Charlie lay in bed, unable to sleep? The old Charlie wouldn't have gotten up, even then, to see what she was doing; he would have been too afraid to. He would have just laid there until she came to bed—whenever that was—and stared at her while she slept. Sara Sue was prepared to deal with that complacent, passive, nonconfrontational man. She had no idea how to work with this one, though, this guy who made a surprise visit home in the middle of the day, this guy who looked like he might know a little something but didn't want to say—not because he was afraid to, but because he didn't want to... yet.

So... what now? Should she lie there until Charlie wanted to get up or should she get up first? Should she start talking a little or would pillow talk get her into more trouble? Cooling her heels like this was killing her. Sara Sue wanted to get back out there. She had research to do, a killer to find. Lying in bed wasn't going to help. What did they say? That the first 48 hours were the most crucial? If so, she had already wasted half of them.

She stretched her legs, letting her feet touch Charlie's calf, moving just enough to wake him if he had fallen asleep. The old Charlie would have been out like a light, but then, she wasn't dealing with the old Charlie anymore, was she? Today his breathing didn't sound the same, his chest wasn't rising and falling with the same rhythm it usually did when he was asleep. Charlie was wide awake.

Why?

Five minutes go by.

Ten minutes.

She had to do something or else she'd be stuck there until nighttime!

"So, what are you doing for the rest of the day?" Sara Sue asked, hoping it didn't sound like an invitation to be with her. Would he really blow off work and drinks with the guys? She hoped not.

Charlie hesitated.

Not normal.

Sara Sue was starting to get a little unnerved. None of this was normal at all.

"I've gotta get back," Charlie said, after what seemed like an hour. He was looking up at the ceiling while he talked, his mouth close to her forehead. She could feel his warm breath on her skin. It was nice.

"I have a job I can finish early if I dig in today," Charlie said as he swung his legs over the side of the bed. "But I'll come home after work instead of hanging out tonight."

Charlie got up from bed slowly, like he didn't really want to. Some part of Sara Sue didn't want him to either. She wanted to hug and kiss and stay in bed with him all day. The sex was good, but it wasn't just that. They had gone back in time for a little while. She had liked it there. But at the same time, she needed to get up and get out. Tina's murderer was still on the loose.

She watched Charlie dress, savoring the view of his body from the bed. It was like she was seeing him for the first time. Charlie was still a good-looking man.

Charlie leaned over the bed, kissed her forehead, and said goodbye. Before leaving the room, he said, "I'm glad I came home today, Sara Sue. I'm glad you were here."

There went that boyish grin again. She could get used to that.

"It was really nice."

Then he was gone. A few seconds later she heard the front door close and then his engine purred to life.

Sara Sue laid in bed after he left, thinking about what happened, going over everything she and Charlie said. She didn't think she had given anything away. She also didn't think Charlie was completely convinced, but he didn't have anything to go on, so she hoped he would just drop it. It was hard enough trying to just be normal and live life while keeping what she had seen under wraps. It would be really hard to hide it from someone who was looking for something, even if they didn't know exactly what they were looking for.

CHAPTER 21

Charlie hoped Sara Sue wasn't watching him from the window but he was afraid to look up to find out. He didn't have a reason for doing what he was about to do and he couldn't think of a good enough lie to get him out of trouble, so all he could do was hope.

Sara Sue's car was parked closest to the house—her normal spot. Charlie walked around her car, making sure to keep his approach soundless just in case Sara Sue was listening. He turned off the alarms to both cars simultaneously then he opened the driver side door of his car as quietly as he could and left it open a little so the alarm would reengage. He then opened Sara Sue's passenger side door.

He had to be quick.

The camera wasn't on the seat or on the floor.

There wasn't anything out of the ordinary in there—no scrap of paper with phone numbers on it, no printouts of nasty pictures, just receipts for car service, directions to his cousin's house, which he had put in the center console himself years ago for their summer trips to the country, and napkins stuffed into the holder on the side panel. It was messy but normal.

Charlie started to open the glove compartment but decided not to because maybe he was blowing things out of proportion. Maybe he was being paranoid. Either way, Charlie was starting to feel a little silly.

And he'd been out there too long already.

Charlie stayed crouched as he slipped out of Sara Sue's car. He slammed the door shut, jumped into his own car, and pulled his car door as close as he could, hoping it would look closed if Sara Sue decided to look out the window. He used the rearview mirrors as he backed out of the driveway, keeping his left hand on the door. He slammed the door shut as he put the car in gear, hoping it sounded like it was coming from someone else's house.

As much as he wanted to, Charlie couldn't make himself look at the window to see if Sara Sue was watching.

CHAPTER 22

Sara Sue had about four hours to play with before Charlie got home from work and she wanted to make the most of them.

She wrote down the things she already knew.

1. Tina was from Falls Junction. *Was she a small-town girl who partied too much with the wrong crowd?* That was something to think about. Even small towns like Falls Junction, which was far enough from the city to be considered the sticks, had a seedy crowd— people who had drug issues, alcohol issues, or whatever else they thought trendy city folks were doing.

2. Tina had a boyfriend who went to college in DC, which is only an hour-and-a-half drive away from Falls Junction. The boyfriend could have come to Falls Junction and killed Tina and had enough time to get back to DC to go to the first party of the night. Or he might not be involved in Tina's death at all. He could have just stayed home, but what college-aged guy stays home on a Friday night? If he was like most college guys, even if he'd had a cold he would have still gone out if there was liquor involved. So, if

he said he was at home, he was full of shit. This guy might be someone to look at.

3. There was a MySpace tribute up about Tina. Need to look at that. The killer might comment there, say something related to what happened in the park. It was a long shot but what if?

Sara Sue read her list over a couple times. It was good. She wondered if the police made lists when they investigated cases. Maybe there was a new career in this for her.

Sara Sue, Detective.

Yeah, right.

Sara Sue decided she would go back to Falls Junction, maybe back to the park where Tina died. That sounded right. That's what they would do on *Law and Order*. But first she was going to take the camera back to Karen.

CHAPTER 23

Karen was in a talkative mood. She ate up an hour of Sara Sue's time telling her about the guys who had sent her notes on the dating site. She had been so excited to get her page up that she used an old picture instead of waiting for the camera. Sara Sue was happy for her, but she didn't want to hear about it right then. She had more pressing things to do than look at pictures of men in their 40s trying their best to look appealing. But she did it anyway because Karen was her friend, and because she couldn't figure out a reason to give for leaving.

Truth be told, it was fun. Together they picked three guys who looked interesting and responded to them. They talked about Sara Sue's hair—Karen loved it—about their next girls' lunch, and about the sex she and Charlie had just had. Sara Sue didn't tell Karen why Charlie came home early or anything else about what she had been up to. Maybe when the whole thing was over, she could tell Karen and Charlie what had been going on, but not before then. For now, the less they knew, the better.

Sara Sue spent way too long with Karen. By the time she headed toward Falls Junction, she only had two hours before

Charlie was due home. Was that long enough to find the park again, do whatever she planned to do there, and then get back to the house before Charlie walked in the door? Probably not. And she couldn't come out after he got home. Even if she could come up with an excuse to run out, it would be dark soon enough. Did she really want to be at the scene of a murder in the dark? What if the killer came back for some reason—to reminisce about the night, to celebrate, to kill someone else... who knew? What if he recognized her car? What if he decided to kill her next?

Sara Sue turned around and went home instead, deciding to do her sleuthing a different way. She turned on the computer as soon as she walked in the door. While it was booting up, she put her own camera in her purse so she would have it when she went to the park the next day. She'd figure out why she needed it when she got there.

Sara Sue settled into the chair in front of the monitor. MySpace wasn't a website she visited a whole lot. She might have been there once or twice looking at pictures of people she knew in high school, but she hardly knew her way around. She loaded the web page and looked around a bit. She tried to find a page for Lover but they didn't have one. She guessed the old heads didn't care enough to make a page for them and kids didn't know who they were. It was probably just as well—Sara Sue wasn't there to reminisce.

She looked at her watch.

What little time she had left before Charlie got home would be eaten up if she kept playing around.

Sara Sue typed "Christina Tally" in the search field. The memorial page was the first of a long list of hits that either contained "Christina" or "Tally" in the title. A black background watermarked with a picture of Tina popped onscreen. In the picture, Tina was sitting on the beach, her sun-kissed hair blowing in the wind. She was tan; she was young; she was alive.

But not now.

The guilt Sara Sue felt was so heavy, she almost couldn't breathe.

She read the About section... it took a while, but she got through it. Someone had written a wonderful tribute to Tina. She had graduated high school and gone to a community college in Collin Park, where the mall was. She had wanted to go to a four-year college to study psychology, but she had been taking it slow since she was paying her own way. Tina had worked in the mall and also at a dentist's office doing record keeping. She'd had two dogs and a cat, gave money to the ASPCA, and had volunteered at an animal shelter.

All the really sweet ones get screwed, don't they?

Sara Sue skimmed the rest of the page. Reading about Tina's family and how much they missed her wouldn't help Sara Sue with her investigation. It was the kind of thing that would hurt more than help; she could easily get lost in it all, get beaten down by guilt. She would deserve to feel that way, but it would throw her off track. Sara Sue needed to do right by Tina, this girl who didn't deserve what she got.

She had to stay focused.

Sara Sue jotted down that Tina had a brother in his mid-20s and some male cousins, all living in Falls Junction. Could any of them have killed Tina?

Sara Sue noticed that a video had been posted. Reluctantly, she clicked play. Tina popped onto the screen wearing a cropped top and jean shorts. She was in high school in the video, all smiles with braces covering her teeth. A metal mouth. Sara Sue wondered if she had gotten teased about the braces. Then she wondered why she was so frivolous, hating how callous she seemed.

The video was short; it was just Tina doing a cartwheel in gym and landing in a split. There was another video beneath that one of her and a bunch of friends waiting in line in front of a club they barely looked old enough to get into.

Just the exploits of a regular, sweet, young girl.

A young girl who happened to be dead.

Sara Sue needed air. The images of Tina, smiling and happy, made her sick to her stomach. She walked out of the bedroom and crossed the house to the glass door that led to the deck off the entrance to the kitchen. Charlie had been so excited to have the deck built last year—he had been like a kid in a candy store. He designed it himself, made it multilevel with stairs leading out onto the lawn. It had baroque balusters, stone post covers, and a gazebo. The thing spanned the entire width of the house. It was truly a production, and Charlie adored it. They ate on the deck almost every evening that summer. Sara Sue let her mind conjure up memories of the porterhouse steaks Charlie used to make and the skewered shrimp he fussed over, marinated and grilled to perfection. The thought of food pushed the images of Tina aside, if only for a minute.

But they also made her realize she was hungry.

Sara Sue pulled out a of couple steaks, seasoned them with Charlie's special blend and put them in the fridge. Maybe they could keep the romantic momentum going.

She went back into the bedroom and looked at the computer from across the room. She knew she needed to sit down and read the rest of the page—there was more information to be found there, more work to do—but she didn't want to see anymore. Seeing Tina when she was alive and vibrant cut like a knife. Only she and the killer knew what she looked like in those final minutes —only they knew what happened—and she hated herself for it.

No.

Sara Sue didn't have the luxury of stopping; she wouldn't allow herself to.

Tina was dead and it was partially her fault. Sara Sue vowed to keep going, keep trying to find clues and catch the killer. She owed Tina that much.

She sighed as she sat down and looked at the MySpace page again. She started reading the comments, looking for the real nitty-gritty details. The killer might have come to this page, might have left a post. She scrolled to the bottom so she could start at the beginning. Most of the posts were from people who knew Tina from school or work, but there were also some from people who heard about the story on the news or in the paper, expressing their condolences to the family. Some people were angry; they cursed and vowed to punish the bastard who did this if they could ever get their hands on him. Sara Sue printed out the most passionate comments just in case she needed to look into those people. After she had read all the comments through once —all six pages of them—she went back and looked at everyone's picture closely. There was something for everyone; whatever image the person had used when they created their account was right there next to their comment. She tried to think back to what she had used for herself when she created her account. Sara Sue cringed at the probability that she had chosen one of those Sears studio kind of pictures where she was smiling stiffly, head turned at that unnatural angle photographers always asked for, her hand under her chin looking very much like it was propping her head up.

Could the killer be that stupid to use an account that had his picture in it? Maybe. *He* wouldn't think it was stupid, would he? He thought he had been alone with Tina the night he killed her. In his mind, no one was looking at him for any specific reason. He had committed the perfect crime with no witnesses.

Except he *hadn't* been alone.

There were pictures of two guys who looked like they could have been the murderer, but only because they had dark hair that was long enough to mousse into spikes. One was Hispanic, one was White. She looked at the pictures she had taken of the killer: it was impossible to tell his ethnicity from those dark shots.

Great.

Sara Sue read the two guys' comments over and over again. They both expressed their sadness, both said Tina was nice, always there for them—pretty much the same thing everybody else said. Nothing really stood out.

It was a bust.

Sara Sue was right back where she started.

Sara Sue rubbed her eyes and stared at the screen. Was she missing anything? She felt like something was there but she didn't see it.

There was contact info listed on the site, probably for the people who had created the page in the first place. Sara Sue copied it down and put it and the comments she had printed out in her purse, folding them together with the pictures she had taken that night.

Sara Sue googled "Christina Tally," then "Tina Tally." She found a couple of pictures that were completely unrelated to Tina, news coverage of her death from surrounding cities, a blog entry written by a girl who knew Tina in high school. She read the blog and there was nothing of importance there; just a girl sounding off about the murder and how the cops were dragging their feet. A couple people chimed in, replying with a bunch of expletives aimed at the cops, and then the conversation moved on to something else for people to bitch about.

Sara Sue looked at her purse and thought about what was in there, hoping it would help her think of the next move.

What was in her purse? She checked off the list:

- Comments from the MySpace page
- Contact info for the people who made the page
- Pictures she had taken of the killer
- A picture of Tina...

Wait!

She had more than just pictures of the killer in her purse... she had a picture of the license plate too.

Bingo.

Sara Sue took out the pictures and found the one of the license plate quickly. To her surprise, she could make out most of the letters and numbers—only one of them was too blurry to read. She started to feel giddy. This could be the breakthrough she needed. If she could link the license plate to a person, she would be able to find him, get him arrested, put him away. Suddenly she wanted that bastard to pay more than anything else in the world.

She went to the Virginia Department of Motor Vehicles website and found that there wasn't a way to search for license plates there. No surprise. That kind of information can't be available for just anyone to see. People would be looking up everyone who cut them off on the road and go to their houses bent on revenge. Road rage, cyberspace style.

So how could she match a name to the license plate?

Sara Sue took out her list and added another bullet point:

- Have license plate number.

She needed to figure out a way to find out who the plate was connected to without being obvious, without making an impression. There had to be some database, something she could tap into without being noticed. But there was no time to think about it then—Charlie would be home in a half hour.

It was time to cover her tracks.

Sara Sue cleared the search history. Then she surfed a bunch of the websites she normally went to: VideoFitness.com, Epicurious.com, CNN.com, Hotmail.com, Google.com. She even visited websites that Charlie went to. She went back to them all at least three times, each time in a different order. That way, if Charlie decided to be nosy and snoop around the computer to see what she had been up to all he would find was the usual, boring stuff. Before shutting down, Sara Sue looked up concert info for Lover. According to Ticketmaster, there were no dates in the near future.

She printed out a recipe and left it on the desk, sent an email, bought a couple things on Amazon.

All of it bait.

Maybe Charlie would take it.

The old Charlie would have.

CHAPTER 24

Get up and get out.

That's what Sara Sue thought as soon as she heard the front door slam the next morning.

Sara Sue had been waiting for Charlie to leave for work before she got out of bed. She had to make sure he was good and gone and not waiting to go through her purse or the computer or the closet or wherever else he might think to look while she was in the shower. There were too many things to find if he picked the right place.

After a series of stutter-starts, including getting shut down by the DMV when she called and asked about getting license plate information. It was a hard no... something about the privacy act... whatever—and the fleeting moment when she remembered that Karen's cousin was a cop but realized it would do more harm than good to ask for his help (after all, all the stuff she was doing was very much against the law; Karen's cousin might have thrown her in jail right alongside the killer). Sara Sue planned out what she needed to accomplish that day. First on the list was going back to the park where Tina was murdered. She couldn't put her finger on why; when she really thought about it, it seemed like an unnecessary step, but Sara Sue felt drawn to it somehow. Was that how the killer felt? Did he go back to visit the park—the "scene of the crime" as they said on television—too? Maybe she'd see him there, poking around, trying to look like a guy enjoying the sun but not being able to stop staring at the spot where he had left Tina's body, not being able to stop looking for blood or brain matter or some other nasty thing that had seeped out of her while she lay there in the dark waiting to be discovered. Maybe she'd catch him that way.

The thought didn't bring on the hopefulness she had wanted it to.

After she left the park, she would need to figure out how to use the license plate number to identify the driver of the car. If she had the car, she had the killer. She could just go to the police with her pictures and his address and all they'd have to do was pick him up.

Right after they asked her a million questions, the most important two being "Why didn't you call 911 when the murder was happening?" and "What took you so long to say something?"

Sara Sue didn't have answers for those questions, at least not any that would help her plight. She didn't think admitting that she was a coward would be good enough. That she wanted to find the killer to make herself feel human again wouldn't go over well either, but it was all she had.

Which brought her to the last thing on her list: figure out how to turn the evidence over to the police without incriminating herself. She didn't write that one down like she had the others; she didn't think protecting her hide was something she would forget about anytime soon.

Sara Sue read over her task list again to make sure it was ingrained in her head and as she did, she had a thought. A timeline —that's what she needed. Some kind of tracker to keep her feet to the fire. She thought about what that could be—days of the week, cycles of the moon, something. She needed some kind of milestone to call out, to serve as a beacon. And then it came to her. The debut... *her* debut.

It was perfect.

Two days since Tina died.

Four days until Mars.

Sara Sue threw on a white V-neck shirt and jeans shorts, pulled her hair into a ponytail, and put on a baseball cap. She needed to be stealthy today, but it couldn't be obvious that she was trying to be invisible. She scrutinized her outfit in the mirror and changed her mind about the shirt, donning a black one instead.

Casually forgettable.

Sara Sue hopped into the car, a new confidence spurring her along. She was getting close to something—she knew it. All she had to do was follow through on her plan and she would catch that bastard, turn him in, and gain back some of her dignity in the process.

Before backing out of the driveway she fished the picture of the license plate out of her purse.

3LJ48 and some other letter that was too blurry to make out... a D maybe?

Virginia tags.

Who are you?

CHAPTER 25

Sara Sue made her way back to Falls Junction carefully. It was a small town and if she didn't pay attention, she would drive right through it. Joplin Park was right off the main road, past the tiny business district, in the residential section.

She felt weird being there.

There were a lot of people in the park. Several cars were parked in the lot. Sara Sue could see kids playing on the monkey bars, a man and a child playing soccer, a group playing baseball on the field behind the parking lot. The sun was out and it was warm but not stifling hot, the bugs weren't all over her... it felt almost like a day in late spring rather than late summer. Everything seemed perfect; it was almost like a scene in a movie when it was obvious that a meet-cute was coming, maybe on the park bench or in the parking lot itself—except for the memorial that had been set up in the spot where Tina's body was found. Flowers, crosses, posterboards with condolences handwritten on them, candles, and a couple of stuffed animals filled the parking spot and spilled over onto the grass.

This was Tina's hometown and they missed her.

Sara Sue parked at the far end of the lot, not because she wanted to, but because she had to. It was probably better that way anyway—the distance would help her car blend in with everyone else's.

But then she couldn't get out.

She was frozen.

Whatever catalyst she thought the place was going to be wasn't coming to fruition. Instead, Sara Sue felt as if her skin was teeming with bugs, all just under her skin, waiting to break through.

She wanted to leave.

She wanted to leave Falls Junction and everything in it.

She stared at her steering wheel; her head full of noise. What was she doing here anyway? Sara Sue couldn't come up with a good answer to that. What had she planned to get from being there? The body was gone. Even the outline the police drew, if they really even did that the way they showed in the movies, was gone. Nothing but flowers and candles marked the place where Tina was murdered.

What had she thought she would find?

Sara Sue sighed and shook her head. This wasn't the movies. It wasn't as if there was going to be something sitting in the gravel just waiting for her to find it. It didn't work that way. A dog would have carried it off by now or a kid would have messed around with it—whatever *it* was. And even if there had been something to find, Sara Sue didn't have anything to put it in. And what would she do with it anyway—this mysterious evidence that the police had somehow missed? Get a ballistics test? She laughed out loud. She didn't even know what a ballistics test was or if one would be useful in this scenario. Sara Sue had heard someone say it on a TV show one night when she probably should have been asleep; she knew just enough to call up the name of the test from her memory but nothing else.

Sara Sue watched too damned much TV. If she wasn't careful, that was going to get her killed.

Sara Sue looked at the makeshift shrine.

There were a lot of flowers.

A whole lot.

Had the killer brought some? Did he even know about the shrine, that it had been set up in the place where he had taken her life?

Of course he did. He probably drove by it every day. That thought made Sara Sue shrink in her seat.

She wasn't getting out.

She couldn't.

Resigned and disappointed in herself, Sara Sue turned the car back on. She allowed herself one last glance at the memorial. The police had cleared away some of the gravel, probably collected some as evidence. The rest had been cleaned up to spare anyone who came to the park a gruesome sight. New, lighter gravel was in its place, sticking out like a sore thumb.

That's where Tina's blood had stained the ground.

That's where her head had been split open.

Sara Sue left the park feeling silly for having been there in the first place. That little voice in her head sneered, *So what's the next bright idea, huh?* And Sara Sue honestly didn't know.

She was quickly realizing that she wasn't cut out for investigative work. She had silly ideas that went nowhere and couldn't think five steps ahead. But she *had* to do this; she had to see it through.

It was as much for Tina as it was for herself.

As Sara Sue drove out of the park's lot, her thoughts turned to the boyfriend. If she could find out what school he went to she could drive up and there and check him out.

She needed a name.

CHAPTER 26

It was stupid to try the same thing again, but maybe that's why it would work.

Charlie pulled into the driveway at 12:30—right in the middle of the workday. Sara Sue wouldn't have expected him to come home twice in the same week... at least he didn't think she would. So, maybe she had gotten sloppy and left things lying around. Maybe she thought she'd have time to clean up—hours of time. Maybe he could catch her with her pants down.

But not literally. No, Charlie didn't think he could handle that.

Sara Sue wasn't home, and that was a good thing. Charlie didn't think he could handle walking in on her with someone. He was afraid he'd kill the guy. Really. You never know what you'll do in situations like that, but Charlie had a pretty good idea, and it wouldn't be pretty.

He went into the house and closed the door. He scanned the living room and dining room; nothing was out of the ordinary. The kitchen was clean, all the dishes washed, just like Sara Sue liked it. He walked through the rest of the house before approaching the bedroom. Everything was where it was supposed to be. The bed was made, as usual. Nothing, like a lewd photo or a phone number, lay on top of it, but that didn't surprise him. He knew once he walked into a neat house that it wouldn't be that easy. He'd have to work for it this time.

If there's anything to find at all, he reminded himself.

Charlie opened the closet, shifted some clothes around on hangers, looked into a couple of shoe boxes, and felt inside folded sweaters.

Nothing.

He closed the closet and went over to the computer. With a sigh, he sat down and booted it up. If there was anything to find, it would be there. Maybe she was having a virtual affair. That still wouldn't be okay, but at least it would mean she hadn't been physical with the guy.

Yet.

Charlie could feel himself getting angry about the idea. *Maybe that's why she didn't want me to turn the computer on; there's some nasty chat between her and him on here!*

The computer couldn't boot up fast enough.

Charlie searched every single folder on the hard drive—hers and his, temporary internet files, downloads, My Pictures, My Videos, the recycle bin, the program files—everything, but he couldn't find a naked picture or a chat transcript.

He went on the Internet and looked at their favorites. The history folder didn't show anything of interest either—just the same sites that they always went to.

Charlie was starting to feel stupid again. And ashamed of himself.

He started beating himself up for going down that path instead of just dealing with the fact that Sara Sue just didn't love him the way she used to. It was easier to think that she was doing something horrible to him, something that gave him a reason to call it quits—a reason that anyone would understand. Or one that would make him look like a saint if he stayed. If Sara

Sue was cheating, it would make it look like she was wrong no matter why the cheating had happened... no matter what role he might have played in it. He wouldn't have to own up to the fact that he had stopped paying as much attention to her, that he had slipped into a routine and stayed there for years. He didn't have to explain that he avoided her when he thought she was upset, came home late hoping she would already be asleep rather than talk about whatever was going on. If she was cheating, people would see the fault in her and leave him out of it, would even feel sorry for him.

It had been easier to paint Sara Sue as the villain, but it had been a lie.

Charlie had to do something to get their marriage back on track. He loved her and wanted her, and that she didn't feel the same way was eating away at him from the inside out. That's always what it was, Charlie realized. He only *thought* he had fooled himself by putting all his energy into catching Sara Sue cheating. But part of him knew all along that there wasn't anyone else, that Sara Sue wasn't hiding anything. Part of Charlie had always known that the real issue was him.

He wanted to do something special for Sara Sue. If their relationship was going to work at all, she had to know how much he loved her.

The last time he did this Sara Sue loved it, so Charlie figured he'd start with something he knew would work.

He was on his way to munchcrunch.com to get some of the flavored popcorn that Sara Sue loved so much, but he only got as far as www.m. Links for MySpace pages popped up in the address field dropdown. It wasn't a site Charlie visited. In fact, he had never been on MySpace before, so they had to be Sara Sue's links. He highlighted the top one and held his finger over the mouse.

Should he look?

He had been willing to invade Sara Sue's privacy before when he thought she was sneaking around behind his back, but he felt differently now, right? He had changed his mind, believed in his wife again, knew he was the one who had to make a change.

Right?

Charlie sighed. If he did this, if he clicked the link now, that would be snooping for the sake of snooping, wouldn't it? He didn't think she was cheating anymore, had talked himself off that ledge.

The highlighted link seemed to taunt him.

He wanted to look.

He wanted to see what she had been looking at.

What was even on MySpace? Profiles of guys? Maybe she met someone on the site and they hooked up somewhere.

So much for trust, Charlie's subconscious spat, but he ignored it.

Just one look and then it'll be over, the other side of Charlie's mind coaxed, and it was right. If he didn't follow the link, he'd wonder what Sara Sue was so interested in for the rest of the day.

Charlie took a deep breath; he was nervous all of a sudden. He clicked the link and Christina Tally's memorial page opened. He read the tribute and a couple of posts. They all said virtually the same thing. People were sad. People were outraged. People missed their friend. Charlie had heard about her murder on the local news the day they found her body. He had paid more attention than normal because things like that didn't happen too much near their little town, so it was kind of big news. He bet most people who went on the page actually knew the girl but a lot of them probably didn't. The world was full of voyeurs, peeping Toms looking in on someone's sadness and getting off on it. Charlie understood that. He guessed there was a little bit of a peeping Tom in everyone, thought maybe that's what rubberneckers holding up traffic when an accident happened were giving in to. Is that what Sara Sue had been doing on that page? Rubbernecking?

Charlie looked at the pictures and watched the video, trying to figure out what might have interested Sara Sue. There weren't any gory pictures on the page, no gut-wrenching details of what she looked like dead. Maybe other people's sorrow was enough.

But that didn't seem like his wife at all.

Maybe Sara Sue knew the girl. Christina had been years younger, and Sara Sue had never mentioned her before, but that didn't mean anything. Maybe she had brought Christina around and Charlie just didn't remember. He doubted Sara Sue could pick his work friends out from a line up. Charlie looked at Christina's picture again and shook his head. No, he had never met her. He would have remembered her. She was pretty—a real looker with a beautiful smile. If Charlie had seen that smile before, he would have remembered it.

So, Charlie didn't know this girl, but Sara Sue did. So what?

Charlie knew he should shake it off, but he couldn't and he didn't know why. He slowed down and read the tribute again. He still couldn't see a connection. He looked at the pictures and the faces next to the comments and didn't recognize anyone. They were all younger, much younger, as in they had just turned twenty and Charlie was well over thirty. Not quite the crowd he'd hang out with. Nor were they Sara Sue's crowd. So, what was she doing on the website?

Charlie sat back in his seat and rubbed the back of his head. Sara Sue always knew he was thinking up something when he did that; she said he gave himself away. Well Charlie was thinking, all right, but he wasn't getting anywhere. At least not anywhere that he wanted to go. But it had to be true, didn't it? That would account for Sara Sue's utter disgust with him more than anything else, wouldn't it?

He had been wrong about Sara Sue, but not the way he thought.

Sara Sue was cheating, but her lover wasn't a man. It was a woman.

Charlie reeled from the thought once he let himself put all the words together in a sentence. She was having an affair with a woman! He wouldn't have thought Sara Sue would have done it, but that had to be what had been going on. Sara Sue seemed to hate him, seemed disgusted when he mentioned sex. Then she came home with a new hair style and manicured nails.

He started to torture himself with memories.

All those trips to the mall...

The nail salon...

All those times she had told him she was going out with the girls...

Charlie had always thought "the girls" were Karen and women she had met at the gym. He'd never thought about it, never cared. Why would he? Sara Sue being with a woman was the last thing he thought would happen. But everything pointed to that being exactly what went on.

Sara Sue was cheating on him with a woman.

And now her girlfriend was dead.

Charlie shut his eyes. He didn't know whether to cry or scream.

Sara Sue—his *wife*—was a lesbian.

There was no way for a man to compete with a woman. In another man, he could see differences and commonalities. It was apples to oranges with a woman.

Charlie was angry. At least he could punch a man in the face, fight it out. With a woman he was left standing there huffing and puffing while they skipped off into the moonlight. And now that the girlfriend was dead...

Charlie snapped his eyes open. He was starting to put two and two together and he didn't like what he was coming up with.

Christina was dead. Since the murder, Sara Sue had been acting weird. He was getting used to her mean streak—it was becoming a part of life. He didn't like it, but at least it was a constant. Sara Sue had become a temperamental woman. He couldn't count on what she would say, but he knew for sure, before the day was out, she would say something that would bite or cut. But since Monday, the day after they found Christina's body in the park, Sara Sue's nastiness had been waning a bit. She had become jumpy. She was hiding things—he was back to believing that now, in a big way.

And then they'd had sex. Great sex. The best sex they'd had in years.

After this girl died.

Charlie didn't realize he was shaking his head back and forth; didn't know he had formed the words until he heard his own voice say them.

CHAPTER 27

"*N*o. *Please God, no!*"

Charlie couldn't wrap his mind around what he was thinking. It wasn't possible. Not Sara Sue. She was a lot of things, but this really seemed farfetched. Yet the pieces were coming together. Not all of them, but just enough to make him wonder.

Had Sara Sue killed Christina Tally?

Charlie shook his head then pinched the bridge of his nose. It didn't make any sense. Why would Sara Sue do that? Then again, why would Sara Sue do any of the things he thought she had done—committing adultery, sleeping with a woman, sneaking around. None of it seemed like the woman he knew, but could he really add murder to the list?

He didn't know.

But there he was, looking at the picture of some girl he'd never met who had been brutally murdered by someone. He had caught the tail end of some true crime show that Sara Sue was watching one night and the guy talking, some kind of detective or official, said something about blunt force trauma being used in a crime of passion. That's how the newspaper described this Christina's injuries. The person who killed Christina had a real problem with her.

But was that someone Sara Sue? Was it his wife?

Charlie turned the idea over in his head. Had they gotten into a fight? Had Christina wanted to break it off and Sara Sue lost control? That didn't sound like his wife at all, but Charlie no longer put any stock into what he thought he knew about Sara Sue, not anymore. Was it the other way around and Sara Sue wanted to break it off but Christina didn't? Did they struggle and then Sara Sue killed her in self-defense? Charlie shook his head—Sara Sue was hardly a shrinking violet; he imagined that whatever happened, Sara Sue had been the aggressor.

Aggressive enough to kill Christina, though?

No. No, he couldn't go that far.

Charlie turned off the computer, but not before he found out when and where the funeral would be. There had to be another explanation other than Sara Sue being responsible, and Charlie was going to find it. What better place to start than the funeral?

CHAPTER 28

Halfway to the mall Sara Sue came up with her best idea yet.

She took a couple of spins around Falls Junction's city center and found what she was looking for—the auditor's office. The memory of waiting in line to pay her uncle's tax bill came to her from out of the blue. If she was right and they still provided that service to people like him who were suspicious of the mail and hid their money under mattresses because they didn't trust the bank, she'd know the identity of the killer within the hour.

Sara Sue got to the auditor's office an hour before closing. She'd been expecting an empty waiting area. No such luck. The lobby was full of grumpy looking people—women with at least two toddlers apiece and more than a few old men. Not a smile among them.

She saw some forms displayed at the main desk. She headed for the display, twisting, turning, weaving like she was navigating a slalom to avoid little hands and little feet. She skimmed the posted instructions that told her how to do everything but what she needed. She thought about leaning into the glass window to ask the person seated there what she needed to do, but there was a line, six people deep, who looked like they wouldn't have taken to kindly to that.

She sighed and was heading for the back of the line when she saw the kiosks set up around the room. She almost sprinted over to one of them and jiggled the mouse. The menu that appeared was basic: just five selections. At the bottom of the list of possible taxes was a link to the Vehicle Tax Bills page.

Bingo.

Sara Sue clicked the link and a page opened with search fields for name, address, VIN #, and license plate number. She opened her purse and took out the photo, hiding it with her body as best as she could.

3LJ48... what? D? P?

She would have to try them both.

She typed in **3LJ48D**.

Nothing.

She tried **3LJ48P**.

Nothing.

Sweat formed at Sara Sue's hairline. She looked at the picture again, gripping the paper harder than she needed to. Not D, not P. She tried the only other letter that made any sense. If it wasn't right, she'd have to try again another day after looking at the picture through a magnifying glass.

3LJ48B.

The page gave way to a white, borderless screen. The computer was thinking. After what seemed like an hour, a new page came up.

Gotcha.

Computer screen listing

Name: Jared Corning

Address: 3426 Carson Lane

Phone Number: 000-000-0000

Sara Sue copied down the information as fast as she could, trying not to draw attention to herself or show the huge grin she had on her face. There was no phone number on file, but she didn't think that mattered. She had a name and an address.

She *had* him!

It was over.

All that was left was to tell the police.

Sara Sue took the information and ran—almost literally—out of the office. She felt like she had stolen something and gotten away with it. Sara Sue got back on the road and headed home. She wanted to be off the street and back in her house where she could really celebrate. She also needed to make sure her black suit still fit.

CHAPTER 29

Charlie was quiet.

It was a heavy silence, thick.

Sara Sue had asked about work and he had given her a cursory, one-word answer. She told him about her class at the gym—making it up as she went along—but he seemed disinterested in the details. When she was done, he asked if that was all she did that day and she lied and said yes. She added that she had milled around the mall for a while, but that was pretty much it. Sara Sue didn't think he believed her. She couldn't read his oddly complacent face.

He must still think I'm fooling around, Sara Sue thought. Maybe their little romp hadn't change things after all.

She mimicked Charlie and clammed up during dinner. If he didn't want to talk, neither did she.

The night dragged on and on. She took a shower, read a little, did a Sudoku puzzle, and watched TV, but time only inched by.

This was hardly the type of celebration she'd had in mind.

Now Charlie was in the basement alone. Sara Sue didn't want to be down there with him; she didn't want to risk spilling the beans by talking and talking, trying to shake him out of his odd mood. She was worried she'd say just enough to get herself in trouble. Sara Sue was lonely for Charlie, but she couldn't be around him if he was still suspicious. He didn't know what to be suspicious of, but his instincts were right: things were not what they seemed. And there wasn't anything she could do to fix that yet.

CHAPTER 30

Three days since Tina died.

Three days until Mars.

It was Wednesday.

The day of Tina's funeral.

Charlie was gone before Sara Sue woke up. That was very odd. They normally woke up around the same time and they ended up in the kitchen together reading the newspaper or watching the news before Charlie went to work. But this morning, when she had rolled over, half asleep, she had found that she was in bed alone.

Charlie didn't have to be at work until 9:00.

She'd woken up at 6:30.

Where had Charlie gone? What was he doing?

Could she ever fix things?

She sat up in bed feeling a sense of loss that surprised her with its intensity. Would she ever tell him about Tina? About how she just sat there and watched her die? Probably not. He wouldn't understand. Nobody would. She didn't even understand how she could have been that cold. So, if telling him was never going to happen, how would Sara Sue prove there was no one else?

And if he still thought she'd cheated, how would they get past it?

Sara Sue got in the shower with that question hanging in her mind. It was a doozey, and one that she needed to think about... but not now. It occurred to her that she'd been saying that a lot about her relationship with Charlie—*not now, I'll handle that later, this isn't the right time.* It better be the right time soon or Charlie was going to walk out the door.

Did she really believe that?

Sara Sue didn't allow herself to answer. Instead, she sang her favorite Lover tune a little too loudly, but there was no one there to care about that. She was singing to an empty house.

CHAPTER 31

Sara Sue got to the funeral home at the tail end of the wake, just before the service. The place was packed. It was as if all of Falls Junction had come out to pay their respects. Some people had come from work—construction work boots and thick-soled shoes had tracked Virginia clay into the sanctuary, dirtying the floor. But others had taken the day off to attend the funeral and were dressed in their best black or blue suits. Funerals were the only occasion Sara Sue had for donning a suit. She didn't know how other people felt in theirs, but hers seemed to close up her pores and suffocate her. Maybe it was being dressed up when she hadn't been in so long that felt funny—she hadn't worn a suit— that very one, in fact—since her grandfather's funeral ten years before, a realization that came clear as she noted the tension in the zipper as it pulled the material closed across a backside that was bigger than it had been the last time said zipper had been in service. Sara Sue pulled at her blouse and shifted her feet enough to look like she was nervous if someone was watching, but no one appeared to be. She just hoped she didn't start sweating before this whole thing was all over.

Family took up the first five rows on either side of the aisle. People formed their own queue, greeting the closest ones to the aisle with a hug, a kiss on the cheek, or a pat on the shoulder before paying their respect to Tina. Most people approached the closed casket that held Tina's body with trepidation, as if they were afraid of what was in there... afraid that what happened to her could happen to them if they got too close.

Some people stayed in the back like Sara Sue did, never approaching the family or the body. She had no intention of going up front and looking Tina's mother in the eye after what she had done. Sara Sue was afraid that if she went up there, she would tell Tina's mother everything. And she wouldn't understand. Tina's mother wouldn't understand that she had been paralyzed by fear. She wouldn't understand that the guilt was eating her alive. She would just see Sara Sue as part of the reason Tina was dead. She would criticize her for not helping her daughter, for standing by and watching while she was murdered. She would accuse her of getting off on it somehow, of wanting to see how it would all turn out driving her actions more than any desire to help. She might hurl insults at Sara Sue, call her every name in the book, imply that she was part of it somehow. She might even physically attack Sara Sue. It would be irrational, at least some of it would, but she deserved the woman's anger because she was right. In the end, Sara Sue hadn't lifted a finger to help Tina and nothing she could say or do would make that okay. So, Sara Sue stayed put, stayed back in the shadows with the other lurkers. She was able to blend in, to look like one of the people in town who felt sorry for Tina and her family but didn't know them well enough to approach. That wasn't far from the truth.

Sara Sue had never been to a sadder funeral than this one.

There were several tributes from the family; Tina's brother, sister, and cousin shared memories from when they were kids. Then there were words spoken by her best friend, who looked like one of the girls who worked in the clothing store with Tina, and some from a neighbor who had known Tina since she was two years old. Some of the stories were long and drawn out; Sara Sue was infinitely thankful that she had snagged one of the few remaining seats when she got there. The congregation roiled with sobs and wailing—there wasn't a dry face in the room as each of the speakers described a wonderful woman in the making; a girl who had done well in school, was working on her future, had friends she had known since they were kids, donated her time, was funny, happy, and living life to the fullest. Tina loved hard and people loved her back the same way. She had plans, had wanted to do something with her life, but now her life was over.

Jonathan Terry, Tina's boyfriend, said he had planned to ask Tina to marry him that coming weekend and showed the ring to prove it.

The room erupted with people expressing their pain.

Tina's mother's chest heaved as she tried to keep herself under control but failed.

Tina's father tried to console her, but her breathing gave way to a hoarse scream.

Tina's best friend shook her head violently and wiped at her face as if a gnat was aggravating her.

Jonathan's mother wept loudly.

Jonathan stood next to Tina's casket, his body visibly shaking. He held the ring out in front of him, his arm outstretched toward the casket, offering it to Tina. It was Tina's father who stood, turning the care of his wife over to his other son, who sat in the seat next to her, and hugged Jonathan before he crumpled to the floor.

The sound of people's grief was deafening.

Sara Sue watched as the two men embraced and the people around the room covered their mouths, shook their heads, comforted each other. Her eyes were wet, but she was also thinking. Thinking about Jonathan. Thinking about the night Tina died. Tina had said someone's name when she was talking to the man that killed her. Sara Sue remembered that now. Sitting in a room filled with people mourning the woman was helping her call up parts of that night that she hadn't thought were stored in her head. The name had finished with what sounded like an *an* sound. Like maybe Jona-*than*. His name fit, but Sara Sue didn't know if Tina had really said the name *Jonathan* or if Sara Sue was just making it work. The name Tina had uttered was on the tip of Sara Sue's tongue; she could hear her voice, could hear her saying most of the words she had said that night, except that one—probably the most important one. And the bad thing was that Sara Sue knew it wasn't because she *hadn't* heard it; most of their conversation had been pretty clear, even from the distance she had put between them. It was because she couldn't remember. Damn it! Why hadn't she written it down?

Because she had been scared shitless, that's why.

Sara Sue kept tossing names around in her head—Aar–*on* (but she had to say Aar-*in* to get it to work), Benja-*min*, Si-*min* instead of Simon, Dami-*en*; she kept rolling them around in her head, trying to see which one worked best. She also wondered how the name she had uncovered at the auditor's office—Jared—came into the picture. Who was Jared? Had Tina been seeing him on the side and been found out? Was that what the discussion in the park was about in the first place? Sara Sue had time to think about all of that —it took several minutes for Tina's father and boyfriend to break their embrace and sit down again.

By the time the service itself began, everyone was emotionally spent. The pastor spoke in generic terms as most of them do when they officiate funerals. The message, however, was beautiful—that death is part of the cycle of living. The ceremony wasn't particularly religious; there was no talk of eternal life, God's will, or seeing loved ones again. Maybe Tina and her family weren't churchgoers or maybe Tina herself hadn't believe in all of that and her family was giving her a sendoff she would have appreciated. Sara Sue didn't know, but it didn't stop the guy next to her from blurting out "Yes, Lord" and "Thank you, Jesus" every time the pastor took a break for air. She wanted to move away from him so people didn't catch her in their peripheral vision as they stole glances at him—and they did... tons of people did because he was hard to ignore—but there was no way to do that without calling attention to herself. Sara Sue just hoped people remembered him and not her.

Sara Sue was so drained when the service was finally over that she contemplated going home instead of following the procession to the cemetery. She made her way to her car as inconspicuously as she could, got in, and sat for a while as people lined up to follow the hearse.

She didn't want to go.

She hated funerals and cemeteries and everything that went along with death. The less she saw of the inside of a cemetery, the better. But she had to go. She needed to look at the people, and more importantly, the cars. She needed to watch Jonathan some more. He looked legitimately upset, but what if he had bought that ring *after* killing Tina, thinking it might be neat if he stirred things up at the funeral? She knew that was unlikely, but if he was the killer, it was possible. And why not? He already had everybody fooled, so why not add another feather in his cap for kicks?

Sara Sue wanted to see Jonathan's license plate.

If Jonathan was the killer and was driving his own car, she had him.

The little voice in the back of her head reminded Sara Sue that the car might not be registered in his name—maybe it was in a parent's name or a cousin's. Maybe the car wasn't his and he was just borrowing it.

Sure... maybe.

Sara Sue didn't know if any of that was true but the one thing that *was* clear was that she needed to go to the cemetery. It was the one place where everyone who knew Tina would be gathered in one spot.

She couldn't miss this opportunity.

The hearse pulled away from the funeral home, followed by two family limousines. She let seven cars get in line before she joined the throng of mourners heading toward the cemetery. She kept the cabin of her car silent; she had turned off the Lover CD before pulling up to the funeral home. It didn't seem appropriate to listen to something that made her happy when Tina could never find that comfort again.

CHAPTER 32

*S*he's here.

She's actually here.

Charlie couldn't stop staring at Sara Sue once he picked her out among the mourners. She had hidden herself pretty well; someone would have had to be looking for her to see her. Well Charlie *was* looking for her and he *did* see her. To him, she stood out as if she were wearing neon yellow and gesturing like a mime.

Why was Sara Sue here?

God, he had wanted to be wrong. If he had been wrong, then maybe he could have salvaged some vestige of his pride, maybe he could have even picked up the pieces of their relationship. But there she was.

But why?

Even after everything he had found so far, he still wasn't sure... wasn't ready to believe. Charlie ran through all the possibilities he could come up with during the service:

Number one: Christina and Sara Sue were friends so Sara Sue was mourning her.

If that was true, why hadn't Sara Sue said anything about her, especially after she died? Even with things being so strange between them, a friend being murdered was big enough news to share. Sara Sue would have told Charlie about it and would've told him she was going to the service. As much as Charlie wanted friendship to be the reason, it just couldn't be.

Number two: Sara Sue was being sensitive about the brutal death of a young girl in a town so close to them. Maybe the whole thing hit home and she felt drawn to it.

Yeah, right, he thought. Maybe if he was talking about some sensitive, empathetic woman, sure, but Sara Sue wasn't that kind of woman. She could be nice, but she definitely wasn't *that* sensitive.

Number three: Christina was a stranger and Sara Sue killed her in self-defense.

Okay...

There were a lot of holes in that scenario that he wished he could fill, but fell short. Every time he answered one question another one reared its ugly head.

What was Sara Sue doing in a park after dark in a town she didn't know?

Sara Sue wasn't a weak looking woman. Why would Christina attack her?

And probably the most important one, if Sara Sue had acted in self-defense, why hadn't she told the police? Or Charlie? Or anyone?

It didn't jibe. It didn't jibe at all.

Number four: Christina and Sara Sue were lovers.

It made complete sense that she would come to the funeral if they had been in a relationship. It made even more sense that she would hide herself in the back of the room, almost in the shadows. Maybe no one knew about Sara Sue and Christina. Christina would've been cheating on her boyfriend as much as Sara Sue was cheating on Charlie, so of course she would want to keep herself hidden, make sure their relationship stayed under wraps. No one seemed to recognize Sara Sue, at least not that Charlie noticed, and he stayed for most of the ceremony. He'd gotten there late hoping that Sara Sue would beat him to the funeral home. He'd banked on her trying to get there early enough to catch the beginning, sure she wouldn't want to miss a thing. And he was right. When Charlie came in, he was able to slink along the wall undetected and watch her from afar.

Well, he was watching and he wasn't sure what to make of what he was seeing. Sara Sue was motionless, stone still, like a statue. She was sitting next to a holy roller who kept shouting ad libs out, getting some of the other mourners going every time. That kind of stuff had never sat well with Sara Sue, and he could tell that she was trying to distance herself from the guy without actually moving. It was working. Given the attention he was drawing, people only saw him and paid no attention to her. She was just another woman in the crowd wearing a boring black suit just like countless others. That's what she wanted, wasn't it? Anonymity. Why? Because the truth would hurt everyone—Christina's boyfriend, Christina's parents, her friends, that's why.

Beads of sweat formed on Charlie's forehead.

There was another possibility. Charlie didn't want to think about this one, didn't know how he'd stomach it if it was true, but he couldn't leave it off his mental checklist:

Number five: Sara Sue killed Christina and was there to watch the result of her handiwork.

Was she enjoying their grief? Was she relishing the sadness that was so thick it was almost palpable? She could stand right in the middle of things and watch because no one knew her. She was just one of the many mourners there to pay their last respects. She could be a woman who worked at a coffee shop Christina went to or someone who got her hair done at the same place Christina did; the family wouldn't know either way. Christina had been a grown woman, someone who knew people her parents didn't know. And if Sara Sue was someone who had come into Christina's life outside of her usual circle, it was possible that family and friends wouldn't know about her at all. Charlie thought about how many people he knew that Sara Sue was completely unaware of—guys at the barber shop, at work, at the gym. Was that what Sara Sue was thinking, that no one even knew she existed? Was she that brazen?

Was his wife standing in front of this girl's family with her blood on her hands?

No. Impossible. Not Sara Sue. It was sick to entertain the idea that she could kill someone, and it was even worse to think she was sadistic enough to attend her victim's funeral.

But what if it was true?

Charlie shook his head before he realized what he was doing and stopped abruptly. He cast a quick glance over at Sara Sue to see if she had noticed.

She hadn't. She was too busy looking at her feet.

He looked at the casket, or at least the corner of it that he could see. He couldn't believe that Sara Sue was a cold-blooded murderer. No, if she *had* killed Christina, it was for a reason, not just bloodlust.

The last possibility was that it had been a crime of passion. It was number six on his list. Maybe Sara Sue and Christina *were* lovers and Sara Sue had killed her during an argument. He looked over at Sara Sue again, thought about how she had been acting over the past few months—the distance and then the shift in affection—and felt his own tears starting to flow. He didn't want to admit it, but he thought he had figured out what happened. He thought Sara Sue had killed her lover and it was tearing him up inside. How could Sara Sue do this to them? How could she just throw their relationship away by getting involved with some girl and then set her own life on fire by killing her? Did she just not give a damn what happened anymore?

Charlie didn't know what to think. He felt as if Sara Sue had been living a secret life while he had just stood there, oblivious.

How many other things had she hidden from him? How many other affairs? How many other lies?

A bigger question loomed in Charlie's mind, one he wanted to ignore but didn't know if he could.

What was he going to do about it?

Charlie thought about that as the ceremony drew to a close. He let Sara Sue leave the chapel before he did. He gave the hearse time to pull away with mourners' vehicles filing in behind it before walking outside. He saw Sara Sue's car in the procession and fresh tears stung his eyes.

CHAPTER 33

Bridgeside Memorial Cemetery was in the next town over from Falls Junction—Rolling Hills. It was old. Old enough that some of the gravesites had sunken headstones decorated with simple crosses that only had hand-chiseled initials marking them. The cemetery was pretty big, though not as big as some of the military cemeteries Sara Sue had been to or the memorial gardens she'd seen in big cities that had so many paved streets that you felt as if you'd driven into a little town. Bridgeside had beautiful, mature weeping willows scattered throughout with graves nestled under them, and marble benches for visitors to sit on; there was at least one bench for every two rows of graves. The cemetery had hills and emerald-green grass. It was like a park, only no one went there to fly kites or play touch football. The only reason to be there was to mourn or be mourned.

Huge stone tombstones with crosses or angels at their points cast shadows on the ground. Cherubs were carved three-dimensionally on smooth marble, faces of the deceased were lasered onto newer speckled stone, lambs topped the headstones of babies. Small mausoleums were mixed in with single graves in some of the older sections; they had ornate doors with family surnames on top of them, wrought iron gates, stone facades. They loomed menacingly, ready to suck someone inside and lock them in. It was no surprise to Sara Sue that the horror genre focused on the dead. This was the stuff of nightmares.

Sara Sue hated cemeteries. This one in particular.

She had spent many an afternoon walking around Bridgeside Memorial Cemetery. Six or seven members of her family were buried there. Her mother said that visiting the graves of loved ones on holidays and on their birthdays kept them alive in your heart. Sara Sue remembered her mother sitting in front of the tombstones and talking to her relatives, telling them about what was happening in the world, what was happening in the lives of the family they had left behind. She would reminisce about things she had done with whomever it was—Sara Sue's grandma, her Aunt Jessie, whoever she and her mother were visiting that day—and her mom would smile. She would laugh out loud sometimes too causing people to look over at her, the sound seeming unnatural in such a solemn place. To Sara Sue, it felt weird to talk to cold stone as though it was a living, breathing person, so she would leave her mother to her conversation and explore. That's why she knew the cemetery had a slave section at the very back of the grounds and a military section with soldiers buried there from the Spanish-American war.

She also knew where there was a dip in the ground so deep it looked like you could fall in and never stop... until you touched the casket underneath.

On one of her walks, she had almost done just that. Sara Sue and her mother had gone to visit her cousin's grave on her birthday, which was weird because they'd never visited her when she was alive—not on her birthday or any other day. Sara Sue had wandered off and started her usual game; she had gone in search of the oldest grave. That day, when she explored one of the overgrown paths in the back of the cemetery, Sara Sue found a grave with a birthdate in 1858. She had been sure there'd be old graves back there; it was obvious that no one had visited that section in a long, long time. Sara Sue had walked carefully, lifting her feet high to get through the tall grass. The stones in that section were hand-made; they were just pieces of rock, really, with hand-carved inscriptions. Most just had initials in the stone; some only had dates. Others had a symbol carved on the rockface. One grave just said, "we miss you."

There was one inscription that was hard to see. Sara Sue had squatted to get a closer look. When she had kneeled to get even closer, her knees had gone down fine but when she had tried to put her hands down, there was nothing below them. She had lost her balance and had begun to fall forward, forward, forward. Her stomach had clenched and her abdominal muscles had engaged as she had tried to stop herself from falling into the hole—into Hell... that's where she really thought she would end up if she couldn't stop herself—but she hadn't been strong enough. She had screamed; she heard her own shrill voice piercing the air, but she had been too far off the beaten path for anyone else to hear her. She had been terrified. Sara Sue had known that if she fell in, no one would have known where she was. And she'd have been stuck there. With dead people. At night.

Her hands had touched rough ground a second or so after that terrifying realization, rocks had bitten into her skin as she had gripped the mouth of the hole, desperate to stay out of it. She had sat up fast, had thrown herself in the other direction, had backpedaled frantically—wanting to get away from the hole as quickly as possible... just in case someone was down there, waiting for her to get close enough, to let a limb dangle so they could pull her all the way in.

Her imagination had run wild.

Sara Sue had envisioned dead people watching as she fell, smiling about it, excited as they waited for her to join them. She had stood up fast, had almost fallen as she scrambled away. Sara

Sue remembered wondering if it had gotten darker all of a sudden of or if the air was suddenly cooler. She had started running before she knew what she was doing, her feet acting on the fear of bodies standing before her in tattered clothes, their flesh rotting off their bones and falling to the ground with wet slaps. She had to get away before she never could.

That was pretty much the way Sara Sue was feeling when she pulled into the cemetery. She couldn't help but look over at the section where it happened. It was still as unkempt as it had been all those years before. She shuddered as she looked away, a memory coming to her unbidden, unwanted. Sara Sue still remembered the name on the tombstone, the one that was hard to see so she had gotten close—too close —to make it out.

Gertrude.

Sara Sue turned onto another path in the cemetery as if she was going to visit a different grave. She hoped the people behind her were too wrapped up in their grief to think about what she was doing. She couldn't run the risk of being noticed at the gravesite, couldn't allow herself to be that exposed. The cemetery was full of great cover—tall and wide tombstones with large print inscriptions and statues of angels pointing to the sky.

She could hide there, among the dead.

Sara Sue parked her car around the corner from Tina's procession and got out. Standing in an aisle between huge tombstones, she was able to see the graveside service clearly. She scanned the faces again. No one looked out of place or suspicious. All the people surrounding the gravesite looked familiar from the chapel—no one new seemed to have tagged along during the drive over, nor had anyone been waiting for them to get there. She looked at the cars parked along the road. None of them looked like the one from that night at the park. A quick scan of the area only showed a couple other cars scattered throughout the cemetery. They must belong to other people visiting loved ones. She wondered if there were any kids out there roaming the place as she once had. She wondered if any of them had been to Gertrude's grave yet.

The cemetery run was a bust.

Sara Sue looked over the mourners crowded around Tina's graveside in despair. No one noticed her; they were preoccupied, each of them too wrapped up in saying their final goodbye to a girl who shouldn't be dead. At least, that's what she hoped was happening. All too easily her mind inundated her with new worries, fresh rings of fire to jump through. What if the police were there, dressed as mourners? What if they had staked out the cemetery and were watching, waiting to see what people would do? She would look suspicious to them, standing away from a procession she had come in with, watching the service from afar. They might be running her plates because of that, gathering as much information as they could to use against her later.

They might think *she* was the killer.

Sara Sue started back to her car, forcing herself to walk and not run like she wanted to. She had to get out of there, but she had to do it without raising any eyebrows.

Only after she had turned out of the cemetery did she feel comfortable. No one came out of the cemetery behind her; she didn't seem to have a tail. Maybe the cops only did that on TV.

Sara Sue settled into the drive and thought about what to do next. First things first, she needed to get out of those clothes. The heels were killing her, the stockings were chafing her thighs, and the skirt was just a little tighter than she remembered it being. Going home first was a must. Then she needed to step things up. She had a name and an address. It was about time she used it.

CHAPTER 34

There she was again.

He was seeing too much of her.

The first time had been the day before, when he caught her hanging around the park. She hadn't gotten out of the car and that's what had made him notice her. She had looked nervous sitting there, her hands gripping the steering wheel so tightly that her knuckles had turned white. He remembered watching her drive away, remembered dismissing her as some kind of freak who liked to show up at crime scenes but was too afraid to actually stand in the same spot where someone had taken their last breath. Then he had seen her at the funeral home looking nervous again, so nervous that he had wanted to sneak up behind her and yell "Boo!" just to watch her jump out of her skin. She was still there when he left; she must have stayed for the whole thing but he left the funeral early. He wanted to get to the cemetery before everyone else to find the perfect hiding place.

And there she was again.

He watched her as she spied on Tina's graveside service from another section of the cemetery. She'd come in with them, but she had pulled away from the procession to watch the ceremony from afar. Why? Who was she hiding from?

Who *was* she?

He looked at her again, trying to place her face but he couldn't. He was sure he had never seen her before yesterday. He wouldn't have noticed her then if she hadn't seemed so out of place. She had been trying so hard to act like everybody else but ended up sticking out like a sore thumb. At least that's how it looked to him. No one else had seemed to notice her; no one sensed anything off. But that made sense; he always saw things in people that others didn't. He had a knack for picking out inconsistencies. A teacher once told him that, and it was as true in mathematics as it was in life. Personality flaws had no chance of staying hidden when he was around, no matter how hard a person tried to cover them up. He didn't always call out people's quirks, but he remembered them, cataloged them for use another day. So, when he saw that woman at the park, he had immediately noticed how unsure she had been, how jittery. It had been funny, really, watching her sit in her car, no doubt deliberating on whether or not she was going to get out or cut and run. But why had she been there in the first place? What had she been up to?

He had been kicking around the soccer ball with his little brother, when she pulled into the parking lot. It had been odd being there... odd, but invigorating. He'd felt electric—as if all his senses were heightened, alive. But no one could tell. He never showed any emotions he didn't want people to see. He had become very good at hiding things.

He and his brother had put a rose on Tina's memorial in the parking lot before they played. It had been his brother Bobby's idea, at least he made the boy think it was. Bobby had always liked Tina and he was sad that she was dead so it was easy enough to lead him to that specific park to play soccer. They could put a flower down for her, he'd said, maybe say a prayer. Bobby had agreed; he wanted to say goodbye in some way, and his big brother had been all too willing to provide one.

Bobby had talked about Tina for the first few minutes of their game too. It had pissed him off, but he didn't let on. To get Bobby into the game and the conversation off of Tina, he had passed the ball high, setting up the perfect headbutt shot; Bobby loved to headbutt soccer balls. And that's when he saw her sitting in her car, trying not to be noticed. He had watched her as she thought she was being inconspicuous and had wanted to laugh out loud. She needed a lesson in sneaking around. He could even teach the pros a little something about being stealthy.

The baseball cap had been bothering her—he remembered that too. She kept playing with the brim, adjusting it, lifting it off her forehead and then putting it back down again. He remembered thinking that the hat was a terrible choice of costume; most women with convertibles didn't wear baseball hats when the weather was warm. He'd had a good laugh at her as he returned Bobby's pass.

He had written her off, but maybe he shouldn't have. The thought tickled the back of his neck like a single hair blowing in an unseen breeze. That's what she had seemed like—just some crazy who wanted to sneak a peek at the place where somebody had died. People like that were all over the place—the ones who get off on gory stuff—so he had just thought she was one of them. After all, that had been part of the reason he was at the park that day too, he guessed. It had given him a thrill to be so close to the spot where he had killed Tina—literally within spitting distance of it. He had wanted to stand over the memorial and remember what she had looked like in her final moments, even if he had to do it under the pretense of saying goodbye for Bobby's sake. But the kid couldn't handle that. Bobby had already been fighting tears when they laid the rose down on top of the other things people had left for her. He had to offered to take Bobby home, had to make himself look as dejected by the prospect of that as he could, to get the kid to stick around for a while. He'd have done it, of course; he would have taken the kid home, if it had come to that. But he hadn't wanted to—not yet. He had wanted to soak up the view a little bit longer, had wanted to imagine he could smell the tinny scent of her blood on the air.

He chuckled to himself. Apparently, he was one of those gore crazies too.

He had forgotten all about her until today when she had shown up at the funeral, but even then, it hadn't really meant anything to him. It wasn't until she had pulled up at the cemetery in that little black convertible that he had really started to pay attention; to wonder. Then she had pulled the biggest dummy move of all— veering away from the procession like she was there to visit someone else.

So obvious, silly girl, he thought. *So incredibly amateurish.*

It was kind of odd to see the same person twice in the same week trying to look as if they were part of the scenery, don't cha think?

He certainly thought so.

He felt something in the pit of his stomach. Fear? Anger? Both? The feeling was spreading, creeping up into his chest, tingling through his arms.

He felt like his limbs, his hands, everything was going numb.

He squeezed his eyes shut, trying to pull himself together. The one thing he couldn't do was get too emotional; emotions were what got people caught.

So, who was that woman and what was she up to?

What did it have to do with Tina?

And why did she make him so nervous?

The woman started walking back to her car, apparently finished with the ceremony even though it wasn't over.

Another bad move.

If anyone else was watching her, they would notice that she was leaving early.

Silly, silly girl.

He, on the other hand, just looked like a visitor to another grave.

He had made sure he was at the cemetery before Tina's funeral procession got there and found a position crouching in front of the grave of James Pritt, Born December 16, 1924, Died December 15, 1999, like he was pulling weeds, pruning flowers, tending house, like a good mourner should. He had time to kill—had gotten there with at least fifteen minutes to spare—time to think about good ole Jimmy Pritt who lay stiff as a board beneath his feet... well, what was left of him did, at least. It was a damn shame to die the day before your birthday. He wondered if James had known it was coming, wondered if he knew he'd never get to see seventy-five— wouldn't get to eat a piece of his birthday cake. Poor sap. Some things were just wrong.

He put down the flowers he had brought for the giver of alibis, which turned out to be good ole Jimmy, and walked back to his car. Or, at least, his car for the day. He'd rented one specifically for this momentous occasion and had planned to return it right after the funeral, but it looked as if he'd be keeping it a little longer than he thought.

There were things he needed to do.

He picked up his pace without looking like he was doing anything more than strolling to his car. He got to his before she got to hers. He waited for her to finish fiddling around—she was probably trying to figure out how to turn her car on without being noticed by the people at Tina's gravesite. He could envision her making that same freaked out face she had made at the park, her fingers clamped on her steering wheel like a vice. He might have laughed if he was anywhere but there.

She sat in the car, deliberating.

He waited.

He didn't think she'd have the guts to turn the car on and go, but then she surprised him. He had to suppress a smile as he watched her leave, letting her get onto the main road in the ceme-tery before pulling out himself. He crept slowly after her, hanging back, waiting to see which direction the silly girl turned. The slow pace gave him a nice, close view of Tina's send-off; of her mother, her father, of a couple of people she had known from high school, of that bitch of a best friend. He knew them all. He hated them all. They didn't know him, would look right through him if they bumped into him on the street. None of them had ever said two words to him, but he still hated them and always would. He was happy they were sad. He was happy they had lost someone they loved. Now they knew how he felt.

He resisted the urge to beep the horn and disturb the graveside service. It would be funny, but it wouldn't be right. His mother had always told him to respect the dead and Tina was most certainly that.

Dead.

Dead as a doornail.

Dead like good ole Jimmy.

CHAPTER 35

*W*hat now?

Charlie had pulled into the back lot of a convenience store down the road from the funeral home after the procession had started on its way to the cemetery, needing a moment to think... needing privacy while he did it. He banged his hands on the steering wheel repeatedly, over and over again until it hurt. His face was hot and tear stained. His jacket was rumpled; it looked like he had left it in the dryer after grabbing at it so much, wringing it in his hands. He was a mess.

How could this be happening?

How could Sara Sue have killed someone?

How could she have cheated on him?

She threw me away.

The little voice in his head kept repeating that poisonous little truth nonstop, like a mantra.

She threw me away.

She threw me away.

But it was more than that, wasn't it?

Sara Sue had thrown her own life away as much as she had cast their relationship aside. She was ruined. It was over for her. If the cops found out she was the one who had killed that girl, Sara Sue would spend the rest of her life in jail. Or face the death penalty. Even if the police never caught on, it's not like Sara Sue would live life scot-free. She'd be looking over her shoulder forever, worrying that some clue would be uncovered that would point to her. If she ran, she'd be running forever.

Sara Sue's life, as she knew it, was over.

And so was his, if he planned to stay with her.

Charlie shook his head and leaned into the steering wheel. That was the question; did he plan to stay with Sara Sue?

A murderer.

An adulterer.

His wife.

The love of his life.

She threw me away.

Charlie wanted to have kids with her. They hadn't talked about it recently—hadn't talked about anything at all for the past few months—but he had been planning to bring it up, to wear Sara Sue down, to work on her, to soften her to the idea. But then all this started, her nastiness, her disdain.

Her affair.

Charlie had wanted to move into another house—a bigger one somewhere warmer so he could cook out all year instead of just for a couple of months. He wanted to travel with Sara Sue, have sex on a beach, swim naked in the ocean with her, live life with her.

Now all that was gone.

Unless he could prove that Sara Sue didn't do it.

Was he willing to do that if it meant lying? If it meant making up evidence to point away from her? Planting it?

Charlie turned the key in the ignition and backed out of the space, his jaw set. He knew covering for Sara Sue meant all those things and he was going to do them. But he needed to know the truth first.

CHAPTER 36

Sara Sue went home and booted up the computer to find directions to the address she got from the auditor's office. It turned out that the house wasn't far from the auditor's office itself—just a couple blocks away. She leaned back in her chair. Should she go now, right when people would be heading over to Tina's house for the repast, or should she wait until things had calmed down a bit? So far, she'd done a good job of avoiding contact with people who knew Tina. She needed to keep doing what she'd been doing.

Sara Sue chuckled to herself, marveling at how her thinking had changed since she started looking into Tina's murder. She was getting good at all this stealth business.

She turned off the computer and went to the bathroom to turn on the shower. Even though it had only been a few hours since her first one of the day, she wanted another. No, she *needed* it. Sara Sue needed to wash away the funeral, the cemetery, the dread she had felt the whole time about being caught. The guilt. She needed to be clear-headed for what was coming next, and that wouldn't happen if she was bogged down with emotions that couldn't help her.

A shower first, she thought, *then maybe some tea.*

Maybe she'd relax in front of the TV for a little while and sip some Madagascar Red with cream, let her mind settle itself before jumping into action again. What she needed to do would keep, but her sanity wouldn't.

A shower.

Comfy clothes.

Some daytime TV.

Her favorite tea.

The plan was sounding better and better every second.

Sara Sue let the shower run hot. She liked the feeling of pin pricks as the water touched her skin, then the comfortable warmth as her body got used to the temperature. She stood beneath the spray, letting the water cascade down her shoulders, over her stomach, her thighs. It felt good. She hadn't relaxed since last weekend... since before Tina was murdered.

A lifetime ago.

She closed her eyes and let the water run over her face, let it wash away the funeral and the graveside ceremony, let it wash away her worries about Charlie and what was going on in their marriage, let it wash Tina and everything about her down the drain. It was nice to let go for a minute, to think about the things that used to occupy her mind, like what fitness class she wanted to take next, where the next girls' lunch would be, how Karen's online dating was coming along, what she should make for dinner. All that was easy stuff considering everything she'd been through recently. *That* was the stuff that made up everyday life, not all the stuff she had gotten herself mixed up in, playing detective. Apparently, she needed to have her life turned upside down to respect it.

What she wouldn't give to go back to her old life, predictability and all.

Sara Sue let the water massage the back of her neck as she thought about what the next book might be for her book club. It felt like forever since she'd thought about that. She was hosting the next meeting and was late getting the selections out. She probably had a slew of emails from book club members asking what the two choices were, emails the hunt for Tina's murderer hadn't given her time to read. She tried to remember the titles of the books she was considering. There was the new John Grisham and—

BAM

Her eyes snapped open and water dripped into them, blurring her vision.

BAM

Her breath caught in her throat as she froze.

BAM

Jesus, what the hell was that? It sounded like it was close—like it was inside the house. Sara Sue stared at the shower curtain, eyes peeled, waiting for the sound to happen again. It didn't disappoint.

BAM

Louder still.

She shrieked that time.

Sara Sue turned off the water and got out of the shower, pulling the curtain back as quietly as possible, and snatched her towel off the hook.

It's probably just the wind.

Isn't that what they say in horror movies?

Sara Sue was home alone most of the time, but nothing had ever spooked her like this. She even watched scary movies in the middle of the night when Charlie was out with the boys and nothing made goosebumps rise on her skin like this sound did. So why now?

She was scared for the same reason she had been the first night after Tina was killed.

Because the killer might be coming for her next.

But he didn't know about her... right?

BAM

Sara Sue tried to convince herself of that as she dried off and threw her clothes on, but it was a losing battle. What if he did know about her? What if he was watching her? What if he had been watching her the whole time? What if he thought it was funny—this stupid girl from the burbs trying to solve a murder, sticking her nose into things that had nothing to do with her? He was probably toying with her right now, trying to spook her. As much as she hated to admit it, it was working.

How does he know where I live? Sara Sue wondered, panicked.

He must have seen her that night, must have noticed her car. He probably took down her license plate number and did the same thing she had done to get his address.

The room seemed to darken when understanding set in. If he had been watching her, he knew everything she knew. That meant he knew she had his full name and address. He was there to make sure she couldn't use them.

Oh my God! What am I going to do?

A bunch of things ran through her head at the same time, but she couldn't wrangle any of the ideas to use. She wished Charlie was there to help her, but at the same time, she was glad he wasn't. That way he wouldn't die too. He didn't deserve to be hurt because his wife was out there playing games while he worked. That's what it had been, right? A game. She didn't have any business looking into this murder, just like she hadn't had any business following Tina that night. What happened was going to happen whether Sara Sue had been there or not. Her presence hadn't changed anything.

She should have minded her own business and gone home.

She should have been nicer to her husband.

She should have been happy with her life. A lot of people would have loved to be in her position, but she'd had the nerve to whine and moan and act like the world's biggest bitch about it. Look where it had gotten her. Cowering in the bathroom, hiding from a murderer.

She was a sitting duck.

Sara Sue started moving, her arms going everywhere at once,

grabbing for the doorknob, pulling down the shirt she had wrestled over her head. She was about to open the bathroom door when she caught a glimpse of her eyes in the mirror. They were wild, just like her hair was. But worse, they were unsure. Did she really know his name? What if the car he was driving that night wasn't his? What if the name and registration she had wasn't his? If his father or brother or someone else owned the car, the information she had wouldn't be correct. There would be no way for the police to know who the guy was if he killed her too.

BAM

She had to do something. Call the police, get a weapon, Something! She opened the bathroom door slowly and slid out onto the floor, pressing herself flat as she slithered like a snake toward the kitchen. She could kill two birds with one stone in there: use the phone and grab a big-ass knife.

BAM

If she made it in time.

BAM

This time the sound seemed like it was coming from above her. Was he on the roof?

Were all the windows shut? She and Charlie never went into the guest bedrooms unless they had people sleeping over; their three-bedroom, two-bath house had seemed too big for them once they got all their stuff moved in. What if a window in one of the guest rooms was open? The killer could come right in, be in the house without her knowing. He could wait her out, make her think he's gone, and then slit her throat in the middle of the night.

BAM... then a new sound... footsteps, maybe?

Was he coming in?

Sara Sue heard herself make a low yelping sound but ignored it. There was no time to sit and cry about her situation—if she did, she'd be dead.

Sara Sue made her way out of the hallway and into the main room of the house as quickly as she could. She looked around fast, her wet hair sticking to her cheeks as she whipped her head from side to side. She had gone too far. She was out in the middle of the floor with nothing to hide behind. If he came in through a bedroom window or up from the basement now, she would be an easy target. But sliding around on her stomach was harder than she thought it would be. She'd gotten that far on pure adrenaline, but now that she'd stopped, fear crept in and she was stuck.

Frozen.

More of that new sound. She was almost certain it was foot-steps now.

BAM

You stay, you die.

Sara Sue lifted her torso off the ground but stayed low, more Komodo-dragonish than snake now. She made it to the other side of the room faster than she ever thought she could and hid behind Charlie's easy chair—the biggest thing on that side of the room. But doing that meant she'd had to retrace her steps, lose ground. The kitchen was only a couple feet away but getting there meant she had to go out in the open, be vulnerable again. The thought frightened Sara Sue to her core.

She breathed deeply once, twice, three times.

She couldn't stay there, she knew that.

Sara Sue crawled out from behind the chair tentatively, wanting to go back but knowing she shouldn't. She did her crawl/walk as quietly as she could. She'd be on the tile floor of the kitchen soon and she didn't want her hands to slap against it and give her away.

BAM

BAM

He was still outside, stomping on the roof, trying to make as much noise as he could. She thought he was going to come in any second. Maybe he'd pick a rock out of the yard to smash her head in like he had done to Tina. Tina's ruined face flashed in her mind and tears sprung in Sara Sue's eyes, stinging them before they rolled over her eyelids and streamed down her face. She didn't want to die like that. She didn't want to die at all.

Sara Sue vowed to give the whole thing up if she made it out of this. She'd send what she had to the police anonymously and get on with her life. She would make things right with Charlie; she'd show him she loved him and stop acting like such a bitch. She'd be different, thankful for each day. She knew that sounded like what everyone said when the shit hit the fan, but she meant it.

She had to get out of this.

Sara Sue lurched up and forward, throwing herself onto the kitchen floor. Her hands made a loud slap and she froze. Did he hear that? Did he know where she was? Her tears hit the tile and formed a small puddle. She was dead. She knew that now. It was all over. It was just a matter of time.

The front door opened and Sara Sue's heart jumped into her throat. She got up from the floor and ran into the kitchen proper, propelling herself over to the knife set on the counter. She grabbed the chef knife and knocked all of the others out of their block. They hit the floor with a clatter. The phone was too far away, mounted on the far wall near the stove. She'd have to show herself in the open doorway to get to it.

And what if he had a gun?

Sara Sue backed her way into the farthest corner of the room, only realizing when she got there that it might not have been the best place for her to wait. She should probably be at the entrance of the door, off to the side, to try for the element of surprise. But it was too late now. She'd made a mistake. She hoped it wasn't the last mistake she'd ever make.

The blade of the knife caught sunlight from the window, reflecting it onto the wall in bright flashes. If he didn't see her dive into the kitchen, if he hadn't heard her hands and feet slapping against the tile, he sure as hell knew she was in there now. She planted her feet and pointed the blade toward the entrance. There was nowhere to hide, nowhere to run. She had to stand and fight.

CHAPTER 37

As he was coming in the front door, Sara Sue seemed to come from nowhere and run into the kitchen. At least he thought it was Sara Sue—she was moving so fast, he couldn't really tell. Where had she come from? Had she been on the floor? Charlie closed the front door and turned back to the kitchen. He heard a metal clattering sound, like something falling off the countertop.

"Sara Sue?" he called as he walked toward the kitchen a little faster than normal.

He didn't expect to see what waited for him there.

Sara Sue had backed herself into the far corner of the room. She was holding a knife. She was shaking like a leaf but her feet were planted and she had a look of determination on her face.

"Honey?" He tried to speak as reassuringly as he could. "What's that matter?"

Sara Sue seemed to look right through him. She stood firmly in place, not moving. It was as if she didn't recognize him and hadn't heard him speaking.

"Sara Sue, it's Charlie. What's the matter, baby?"

She looked at him then—really looked at him. Her grip on the knife loosened and the knife fell to the floor, the *clank* against the tile sounding louder than it should have. Her face collapsed and she crumbled to the tile right beside the knife, sobbing.

Had Sara Sue had a mental breakdown and Charlie just hadn't noticed?

Was that what had been going on all along?

He couldn't help wondering about that even as he rushed over to her. He wrapped his arms around his wife hoping it would calm her down. She looked wild, crazy. Her hair was all over the place and wet, as if she had just gotten out of the shower, yet she had been standing in the kitchen gripping a knife for dear life when he walked in. He had never seen that wild-eyed look before. Did something in her snap? Was the funeral the last straw? Had whatever had been holding Sara Sue together finally given way to this violent, manic person?

Charlie felt his back stiffen. If she had lost her mind, if some other personality had finally taken over the Sara Sue he knew, he might be in trouble right then. He used his foot to nudge the knife out of reach. Who knew if she would slip into the same trance she had been in a second ago and stab him?

Charlie cast a quick glance around. Everything seemed to be in place; nothing seemed out of the ordinary, except the knives spread out on the floor. Sara Sue was trembling; she was clearly afraid. What had spooked her?

"Sara Sue, what's wrong? What happened?" Charlie pulled her away from his chest and made her look at him. "Tell me what happened."

Sara Sue wiped her wet cheeks and pushed the hair that was sticking to her forehead away. Charlie almost asked her again, but she finally spoke. "You didn't see anything?"

Her voice was weak and quiet. She sounded like a sad little girl. "See anything like what?"

"Outside. On the roof," she cast her eyes up to the ceiling and seemed to cower at the same time. It was unnerving to watch his wife's mind unravel.

"You didn't see him?"

Charlie looked up with her. It was just a reflex. He knew there wasn't anyone on the roof. He could see the front of it from the driveway and would have noticed if someone had been standing there, not to mention the ladder that would have to be propped against the house.

Or would he have?

Charlie didn't remember looking up at the roof—who would? It's not something he would do unless he had a reason to, was looking for something specific. Though he didn't see a ladder—that would have caught his attention—one could have been propped up at the back of the house instead of the front.

His stomach dropped.

He stood up. Sara Sue protested, but he did it anyway. He felt incredibly vulnerable—like eyes were boring into his back—and had to make sure there wasn't anyone out there. Even though he thought it was all in Sara Sue's head, he had to be sure.

Charlie walked over to the window in the kitchen, the same one Sara Sue left open in the summer to yell out to Charlie when he was grilling and peered out.

Nothing.

No ladder, no man standing in the yard.

He halfway expected someone to be there, just standing with his arms at his sides like Michael Myers did in *Halloween*.

Sara Sue's fear was infectious.

Charlie almost laughed but caught himself before letting it out. Who knew how Sara Sue might react to that? He didn't need to spend the next ten minutes explaining himself on top of everything else that was going on.

"There's nothing out there, baby. I don't see anything."

Sara Sue's face crumbled and new tears rolled onto her cheeks. Charlie knelt and cradled her in his arms as she buried her face in his chest. He rubbed her hair and held her tight. He was kind of ashamed, but he liked that she still needed him for something. He enjoyed the way it felt to hold her close, to console her. He wanted to be there for her and if this—the crying, the delusions—were part of it, then so be it. She might not know it yet, but she needed him for a lot of things, and he would be there to help her. He was her husband. Period. Through thick and thin. Till death do us part —isn't that what the vows said?

Charlie knew right then that he would do anything to help Sara Sue. Just like a good husband should.

CHAPTER 38

Close call.

He hadn't anticipated the interruption because it was the middle of the day!

He got angry... didn't these people have offices to go to? Meetings to sit in? Aerobics classes to attend? Living in a nice neighborhood like this, he would have thought they did. They didn't live in one of those new, planned communities with a gate and a guard or anything; the houses weren't massive and gaudy. Theirs was two stories, maybe a split-level type, and it was older—he figured over ten years. Trees lined the street; they reached tall and their limbs stretched toward each other over the road. It was comfy, cozy... safe.

Or at least it *had been* safe. But it wouldn't be anymore, not for Miss Nosy. For her, safe was a thing of the past.

If he was right.

He had to make sure she was really tailing him, really trying to find out what had happened to Tina. If she was, he had to stop her. She might stumble onto something that could link him to what happened in the park that night. He couldn't think of what that could be, though; he had gone over that night in his head a million times and didn't think he had left anything around that could screw him. But what if she had found something like a button, or a napkin that he had used to wipe his mouth days before that had fallen out of the car when he got out? Something as silly as that could put a nail in his coffin.

Coffin. How apt.

He couldn't let her screw things up for him. The cops had nothing. He didn't need some nosy bitch nailing him to the wall.

He had followed her home from the funeral easily enough; she hadn't been looking for a tail, at least not the way he would. She hadn't taken any unnecessary turns or detours—the ride had been a straight shot from the cemetery to her door. Easy to follow. Easy to remember.

He laughed out loud, filling the car with his rich baritone. She really didn't know what she was doing, did she? She was just flying by the seat of her pants, being as obvious as she could be. She was just like all the rest of the idiots in the world. They were all sheep. Most people let themselves be lead from one place to another, oblivious to what was around them and powerless to protect themselves from it. This was going to be easy.

If he was right.

He had some homework to do, a little digging of his own. This was nothing to rush into. Another murder would only make things harder for him, even though this one would be a couple towns away from the first and he didn't know anyone who lived there or that had any connection to that area. He still had to be careful. So much could go wrong. He might get away unseen but what if he had a hangnail that decided to come off in her blood? Or he could have mud on his shoes from when he and his brother played soccer in the park. If any of it dropped from the soles of his shoes and embedded in her carpet, the cops might start thinking broader... might try to make the connection.

Anything could happen.

He didn't want to give the police any reason to look at him. He had succeeded so far with Tina. Those idiots, no better than the rent-a-cops at the mall, were twisted in knots. But even a broken clock is right twice a day. Another murder so soon after Tina's, even one a couple of towns over, would raise a red flag. Their little slice of the world was normally quiet; he couldn't remember the last time there was news of a murder in the paper. He didn't need to be impulsive and mess things up because of Miss Nosy.

But if she needed killing, he would happily oblige.

He so wanted to. His hands were itching to feel the skin of her neck, to tighten around it and squeeze. She wasn't all that hard on the eyes; watching her die might be a turn-on. He messed up that high with Tina. Bloodying her face the way he had, he killed the hard-on he was getting in a hurry. He could hardly look at her after he had bashed her head in, and that pissed him off. He'd do it differently this time; he'd keep her face intact so he could watch her, so he could remember how she looked when she took her last breath.

Little Ms. Busy Body had pulled into her driveway and gotten out of the car without so much as looking around. She had no idea he was there, just a few car lengths behind, watching her as she opened the door to her house and went inside.

He should have left then and he knew it, but he hadn't wanted to. He had wanted to scare her a little, watch her squirm. He had known just how he wanted to do it, too. He had known he wouldn't be able to see her fear—had known better than to get too close too soon—but he'd known he'd be able to sense it. And he'd known she would be scared. Very scared. He had imagined her nipples hardening as her body responded to her fear, adrenaline brimming over as she tried to figure out what was going on—tried to hide. He had thought of her breasts bouncing up and down as she breathed hard and fast. Would she still be in her blouse? Or only in her bra? He had decided to wait a little while to let her take her clothes off if that was what she had gone home to do. Maybe he'd catch her between changes and she'd be topless or even naked. *That* had been a nice image.

He'd waited fifteen minutes then gotten out of the car, which he had parked a few houses up and across the street. Unlike her, he *had* cast a glance around, casually though, like he was supposed to be there. But no one had been looking anyway. He had figured most of those people were at work. Either that or they were too busy chasing rug rats around to notice him. He had walked to her driveway purposefully but not like he was rushing—he had to strike the right balance—and had ducked behind hedges that were entirely too tall. A man lived there. He could tell because a woman living alone would never have let them get that high. She would be afraid that someone would do exactly what he had done. The hedges had provided so much cover he almost hadn't needed to squat down. Men didn't think about things like that; he would feel like he could protect the house and whoever was in it if it came to that. Even if that wasn't a conscious thought, it was lurking in there somewhere. And because of that bravado, getting to the back of the house took less time than it should have.

He'd flattened himself against the house, just in case some housewife looked out of the window, and then it had happened.

He'd heard something.

He had paused—had stood stock still and let himself listen with his whole body.

Water.

She had turned the shower on.

She had left her window cracked *and* turned the shower on.

He hadn't been able to contain the smile that had spread across his face. She was in the shower. He had thought, *This is going to be more fun than I thought!*

He'd looked around for something to use—a rake, hoe, anything, but there hadn't been anything useful in the backyard. At least her husband or boyfriend wasn't stupid enough to leave tools lying around. He'd sighed, casting one last glance around, trying to think of something else to try. There hadn't been much to choose from; the bushes that framed the backyard were mature and there weren't any flowers to speak of, not even potted ones. Miss Nosy didn't seem to have a green thumb.

But there had been something...

It had looked like someone was trying to make a rock garden near the steps for the deck. There had been a pile of rocks, cleaned and gleaming, all different shapes and sizes piled up, just waiting for somebody to do something with them.

He had decided he could make use of those; they would do nicely.

He had picked up one of the smaller rocks first, just to make sure he had the right angle for where he wanted it to land. He hadn't wanted to hit the roof—not just yet. He had aimed for the gutter; that way the rock would hit and stay. Hitting the roof would come later when he wanted to take things to another level, make her think someone was coming after her, their footsteps echoing through the house as each rock rolled down the roof's slant, echoing in her head.

Yeah, that would be perfect.

He had thrown the first rock and it had thundered as it hit home.

BAM

The sound had been richer and louder than he could have ever hoped for. Sweet.

BAM

He had imagined her jumping, startled, just when the water in the shower was starting to feel really good. He had picked another rock of equal weight and threw it.

BAM

Then he had tried a heavier one because why not?

BAM

He had listened again, training his ear toward the open window trying to get close enough to hear a pin drop. She'd turned the shower off. He'd imagined her grabbing her towel and getting out of the shower. She had probably been standing in the bathroom, terrified to go any further, eyes wide and frightened. He had to stop himself from laughing out loud.

He'd waited a little while, letting the suspense build up, and then...

BAM

A bigger rock. Then another.

BAM

And then he had thrown an even bigger rock, but that time, he had aimed for the roof and had watched it roll down. He could only imagine what that sounded like from inside. It excited him to think that she had panicked, certain that he was on the roof, coming in to get her.

BAM

BAM

BAM

He had been having too much fun. So much, that he almost hadn't heard the car pull up. When he had seen it pull into the driveway, he had sighed and sucked his teeth a little louder than he meant to. He hadn't known whether he was more upset that he had almost screwed everything up because he had let his excitement get out of hand, or because he had to stop taunting Miss Nosy. It had probably been a little bit of both.

Damn.

Playtime was over.

As he had listened closely, contemplating whether he should throw one last rock, he had wondered who was visiting her in the middle of the day, why they weren't at work. He'd wondered if she was always home during the day or if this was a special occasion. He wondered about a lot of things that he would need answers to if he was going to do anything else to Miss Nosy.

To throw the rock or not throw the rock... that is the question.

He had figured that if he timed it right, he could lob one last rock onto the roof before making his escape. The person getting out of the car wouldn't hear it if he threw the rock at just the right time—right when the car door was closing. It had been risky, but he'd been game. One side of him had chastised the other for being so reckless. But the other side had told the practical one to shut the fuck up.

The engine had cut off and the car door had opened. He had his rock ready. How long did it take to get out of a car? Three, four seconds if you were not grabbing anything out of the back seat? He had counted the seconds off in his head. *One thousand one, one thousand two, one thousand three...* just like he used to in elementary school. When he had gotten to four, he had thrown the rock...

BAM

The sound of the rock hitting the roof had been drowned out by the car door slamming shut, just as he had planned.

Perfect.

And then it had been time to leave.

He'd stayed close to the house as he had gone back the way he had come. He had heard someone opening the door with a key. Was it the boyfriend or husband? Was it her mother? He'd wanted to look but had known better than to take that risk. He'd already risked enough throwing that last rock.

When the door had closed, he had run for the bushes. He never turned around to see if anyone was looking; he had just walked off their driveway and back to his car. He hadn't needed to look to see whether or not there was an angry face in the window. If they had seen him, he'd have known soon enough, either by a siren or an angry man in his face.

He had gotten in his car and driven off as if he had just finished visiting his dear old grandma. No one had given him a sideways glance, at least not that he could tell. It had been in and out, quick and dirty, and no one knew about it... except her, of course. She had known someone was there. She had known and she'd been scared.

Had it scared her enough to get off his trail... if that's what she had been doing?

Who knew?

Did it matter?

No, not if she had already started digging. If she knew anything at all about him, it was too late for her.

He thought she probably did know something, trusting the hair on the back of his neck that had stood on edge when he recognized her the second time. The idea excited him. The bulge in his pants was welcomed, though he couldn't do anything about it right then. But he'd save the fantasy of her running around her house scared out of her mind for later, when he had time to savor it. He had gotten a taste for killing when he had done Tina. He hadn't known when or if he was going to do it again, but the more he thought about it, the more now seemed like as good a time as any. This woman, Miss Nosy, would be his victim. And what a pretty victim she would be.

CHAPTER 39

Charlie checked the guest bedroom windows four times before Sara Sue would let it rest. She was afraid to be alone in the living room but also too afraid to walk into the dark hallway with him. She stood on the stairs waiting for Charlie to finish, ready to bolt if she had to. He would have found it funny, the way she was so jittery and light on her feet, if it hadn't been obvious that she was completely terrified. Something had scared the hell out of her and he needed to find out what.

"Someone's out there, I know it, Charlie," Sara Sue said from the stairs, but this time he went to her instead of running through the rooms again.

"There's no one in here but you and me, baby. Everything's fine." He tried to put his arms around her but she shrugged him off.

"Don't placate me, Charlie. I know what I heard."

There was the little spitfire he knew and loved.

"Well, there's no one in there now, and it doesn't look like anyone was ever in there. No windows are broken, nothing looks jimmied. Everything looks normal. What do you want me to do?

Call the police and tell them you *think* someone broke in because you heard thumping?"

Sara Sue looked at him as if he had just stabbed her in the heart. Charlie tried to put his arms around her again, and she let him this time. He softened his voice when he spoke again.

"I'm sorry baby, but whatever it was, it was outside. And it's gone now."

He led her to the sofa where they sat, her head laying against his chest.

"Maybe it was debris from the neighbor's yard. They were cutting down that big tree the other day and the wind might have kicked stuff up. There was a breeze when I got home."

It had been a little breeze, definitely not enough to push things onto the roof, but he said it anyway to try and calm her down. Charlie thought Sara Sue might be suffering over what she had done to Tina; she was probably hearing and seeing things that were all in her head. He had to get her to admit what happened and help her move on before things got worse. Seeing her with that knife in her hands had made him realize just how much worse things could get.

"Maybe."

That was all she said. He could tell she didn't believe it. But the truth was, he hadn't seen anything—couldn't explain what she thought she heard—so that was the best he could come up with. Charlie sat with her, silent as he searched for some way to get her to open up.

They stayed that way for a while—much longer than he wanted. It was Sara Sue who finally broke the silence.

"I'm tired, Charlie. Really tired."

Pause.

Should he offer to get in bed with he, hold her as she fell asleep, or keep his mouth shut? Answering that question was almost as hard as the other one that had been nagging at him:

Should he ask Sara Sue if she had killed Tina?

Not if. He no longer thought there was any question about it.

What he should be asking was why.

"Would you come to bed with me?"

"Of course," Charlie said and stood with her. She trudged along in front of him, looking like she could fall asleep at any moment. He rubbed her shoulders as she moved, guiding her into their bedroom gently, slowly. He hadn't pressed her, hadn't asked her the things that were on his mind, the things he'd had every intention of asking when he opened the front door. He'd have to, and soon, if he was going to have any chance of helping her. Sara Sue hadn't asked him why he was home early again either. She would have if she hadn't been scared out of her wits—he was sure of that. Maybe it was good that she hadn't—Charlie didn't have an answer that didn't include him spilling the beans about following her to the funeral. He needed to be sure what he wanted to say before he was forced into responding.

Charlie watched Sara Sue as she undressed and put on her nightclothes; he wasn't thinking of sex, but of how much he loved her. He felt a profound sadness that he couldn't shake, not even when she snuggled next to him in bed, or when she fell asleep with her head on his chest. Something was happening to Sara Sue, his precious love. It was eating her up, turning her mind against her. He had to help her soon before it devoured her whole.

CHAPTER 40

When Sara Sue woke up, it was dark outside. Charlie was still beside her; he'd fallen asleep too at one point, his work clothes still on. For the first time in a long time, she was happy he was there. It felt nice to be in his arms, to feel his warmth. She felt warm. Safe.

BAM!

She couldn't get the sound out of her head. Who had made that noise? Because she knew with every fiber of her being it was a *who* and not a *what* like Charlie had tried to make her believe. It wasn't windy when she got home, not windy enough to move debris big enough to make a noise like that on the roof.

So, who was it?

A neighbor kid? She wanted to believe that and might have under different circumstances; there were a few kids around who were old enough to walk around the neighborhood by themselves and wreak havoc if that's what they felt like doing. But every time she tried to settle on that, to make herself believe it, it wouldn't stick. It was one thing to mess up flowers or throw dirt at houses. It was another thing entirely to climb up to the roof.

BAM

Sara Sue wondered if she would ever have any peace again.

Who had been on the roof?

She thought she knew and the realization made her cold. It was someone from the funeral. It had to be. And it wasn't just *someone*. It was him. She couldn't delude herself into thinking otherwise.

Tina's murderer had followed her home from the funeral.

So, Sara Sue had been right—he did show up to watch the aftermath. But where was he? Where had he hidden himself? She had looked everywhere; she thought she had scanned the funeral and the cemetery thoroughly, but she never saw him.

But he saw her.

He saw her looking for him.

Now he knew someone was looking for *him*.

He had taken action and followed her home. He had followed her *home*.

And...

What was he going to do to her now?

She was afraid of that answer.

Sara Sue thought she was being so careful; thought she had covered her tracks so well. How did he find out about her? She had made a mistake somewhere along the line, one she couldn't remember, couldn't figure out, and it had almost cost her life.

That's it.

She was done—she had to be. The water was getting too hot. She had promised that she would stop if she made it through this afternoon when she had been squirming around on her belly trying not to get killed, hadn't she? She intended to make good on the promise.

Sara Sue breathed a sigh of relief. It actually felt good to know that she was finished with this investigating business and was leaving the detective work to the cops. She would send them what she had and be done with it. Case closed, at least for her.

But would that be enough, or would he come back to finish the job?

No, she was done.

She had to be.

Part of her felt bad about abandoning Tina. Sara Sue had let her die, and now she was giving up the hunt for her killer because she was afraid. She really was a coward. If she had never known that before, she certainly knew it now. Tina deserved better, but Sara Sue couldn't be the one to give it to her. Not if it meant risking her own life.

Sara Sue snuggled closer to Charlie and he instinctively tightened his arm around her. Sweet Charlie. She would have to tell him what had been going on, especially after what happened. She could only imagine what he had thought when he saw her holding that knife. He probably thought she had gone off the deep end. She wondered how close he was to leaving her. But that would all change. Sara Sue was not crazy, she wasn't cheating, and she needed to stop being a bitch. She needed Charlie right now. She had always needed him—she had just lost sight of that for some reason. Everything about them had gotten too familiar, too routine. She needed to change that too.

Sara Sue fell asleep again thinking about how she'd sit Charlie down and tell him everything at breakfast. He'd be mad, but he'd stand by her. Then she'd call the police from some pay phone somewhere far away from the house and tell them everything she knew. Then it would be over. That sounded like a nice plan... the *right* plan.

Just before she drifted into la la land, a hard and cold little voice she'd never heard before whispered in her head,

It ain't gonna be that easy, chica.

CHAPTER 41

Sara Sue woke up, still in Charlie's arms, the room filling with sunlight as it spilled through the blinds. Charlie was already awake and looking at her. She used to think that was creepy, being watched while she slept, but today it didn't bother her. She liked the loving look on his face. Charlie's arm had to be asleep, but he didn't complain. He smiled at her so sweetly when she stretched and yawned, that she almost cried.

This is what love is, she thought.

Today was the day she'd spill the beans to Charlie.

She had to tell him the truth. If she didn't, there would always be something between them, something stopping them from being as close as they should be. He needed to know, once and for all, that she wasn't cheating on him. The only way to make sure he believed that was to tell him what happened. Something as crazy as what had been going on in her life couldn't be made up.

He'd believe her. That was going to be the easy part. The hard part would be getting past the disappointment in his eyes. Maybe there would even be disgust reflected there, and Sara Sue couldn't fault him for that. How would he ever look at her the same way again? Would he understand that she had just been afraid? That she was embarrassed to have been there in the first place and then too frightened to move? Or would he see her for the coward she was?

That's what she thought about while he was in the shower, while she was making breakfast, while they were eating. Charlie engaged her in conversation about the people at his job. It was banal, everyday stuff and it was exactly what she needed. They hadn't talked like that in ages and it felt good, like they were a real couple again.

But still, the worry about what she had to do and what that might mean for them stayed in the back of her mind.

Charlie lingered a little bit after breakfast, probably a little concerned about leaving her. Sara Sue told him to go and have a nice day at work, just the way she used to. She told him she was going to the gym later and after saying it, she actually started looking forward to the idea of a workout. Maybe she'd take a kickboxing class and really blow off some steam. After that, she'd find a pay phone and call the police. She'd give them the license plate information she had, then she'd burn every scrap of paper she had on Tina's murder. And that would be it. She would go home, make dinner for Charlie, come clean about everything, and start her life over again.

But then she started to have second thoughts.

Maybe she shouldn't tell Charlie. He'd look at her differently and she didn't know if they could recover from that.

She had really made a mess of things.

Sara Sue needed things to go back to normal.

She needed to go back to her life and make the most of it.

She needed to do the right thing.

Once Charlie left, Sara Sue started getting herself back on track. She turned on the computer and went to the Internet, deleting her cookies and history, making sure she had wiped away anything relating to Tina. Satisfied, she turned the computer off, showered, and put on some gym clothes. She got all the way to the front door, had her hand on the doorknob, but couldn't turn it.

Sara Sue couldn't move at all.

She was afraid all of a sudden. Terrified. She felt as if someone was right outside the door waiting for her to open it and show herself. Waiting to kill her.

Sara Sue backed away from the front door and sat down on the stairs. She knew she was being ridiculous. She hadn't heard anything—no thumping or clicking or any other odd sounds. She hadn't seen anyone milling around when she had looked out the window earlier. But wasn't that the point? She wasn't supposed to see someone who was trying to hide. She wasn't supposed to hear them if they didn't want to be heard. If he was better than she was at being stealthy, which wouldn't be a difficult feat, he could already be in the house and she wouldn't even know it.

Sara Sue took a couple of deep breaths and tried to reign herself in. There was no one in the house and no one outside. She was just being paranoid, that's all. The whole thing was getting to her and she needed to switch lanes before she lost her mind. That was all it was: nerves. There probably hadn't been anyone outside the day before either. Maybe it was what Charlie had said it was— branches and debris getting tossed around—and maybe it wasn't, but it definitely wasn't a murderer tap dancing on the roof. She was letting the whole thing get out of control.

She had to leave the house. She couldn't be a hermit and hole up because she was afraid of some imaginary boogeyman. The problem was, she knew he wasn't imaginary. He was real, flesh and blood. And he had killed Tina right before her eyes.

Sara Sue stood up and walked to the door with renewed purpose. She opened it and forced herself to step outside. It was a sunny day—it felt like it was going to be nice and hot. It was the kind of day she liked. She was starting to feel better already.

Four days since Tina died.

Two days until Mars.

On the heels of the unwanted timer, she had running in her head tracking how many days since Tina had died and her own life had turned upside down came the countdown that excited her more than she would ever say out loud.

Mars!

The Mars sighting was right around the corner. The scare she'd had pushed the milestone out of her head, almost like it had never been there, but it was back now, in full color. Sara Sue turned her face toward the sun, let it warm her, renew her. She decided she would do something special for Mars night, celebrate it in some way. At first, the Mars sighting was an event exclusively for her because it represented her rebirth, her change, but now it could be for both of them. Charlie might think it was weird and that was okay—she needed to do this.

Sara Sue walked toward her car with purpose, thoughts of blankets and finger foods floating in her head. She and Charlie could put up that old telescope they bought back when they got married in the backyard and sip some wine, eat a little cheese. Maybe she could get some crab legs and chop up some fruit too. Or maybe they could put up a tent and look for Mars naked. It would take a little doing to plan this, but the element of surprise was on her side.

She was excited.

Out with the old, in with the new.

Sara Sue would take care of all the Tina business while she was out and when she got back home, the whole mess would be done with.

There was just one more thing she needed to do before she pulled out of the driveway, left home, and started the business of getting her life back on track—one thing that would round everything out.

Lover.

Sara Sue popped in her Lover CD and turned up the third track. She sat in the driveway letting the tune build, guitars wailing and drums thumping. As loud as she dared to in their quiet little neighborhood, she belted out the words to one of her favorite 80s tunes ever.

Ooh baby
make me smile
make me high
just for a while.
I can't do without cha.
My world revolves around ya.

With a smile on her face, Sara Sue backed out of her driveway and waved to her neighbor who was fooling around in her garden. Sara Sue watched the woman as she put the car in gear. She had the right idea, Sara Sue decided. That was what life is supposed to be after 40. That's what you did when you were officially a grown-up. You got married, you a had a couple kids, you bought a house, you shopped at Super Walmart and Target unabashedly, you grew things in your herb garden at the back of your house—things you couldn't name when you were in your 20s but that you knew everything about in your 40s, like what kind of light it needed to thrive, how much water to give it. You became one of the suburbanites instead of fighting to be different. There's nothing wrong with personal style—Sara Sue was not going to give up her polka dots and bright colors any time soon—but the rest was just a reflection of who she was now. She was married. She and Charlie had bought a house in a suburban area. She got her nails done a couple times a month and went to the gym four times a week. She shopped at Target most of the time. She drank coffee from Starbucks and sometimes she and Charlie went out to eat at some humongous chain restaurant. That was her. Period. She didn't know why she couldn't see the truth in it before.

As Sara Sue drove away, her laughter filled the cabin of the car to mingle with Troy from Lover's singing. It must be true what they said: if you can't beat 'em, join 'em.

CHAPTER 42

The good vibes only lasted a few hours.

It started out okay. Sara Sue had a hard workout and a good hot shower afterward at the gym. Then she went to Starbucks and got her daily fix. She walked around the mall a bit but didn't go anywhere near the store Tina had worked in. Things were going as planned.

Next stop was a pay phone so she could tell the cops everything she knew. She walked to one positioned near a busy entrance thinking that the cops would have a hard time figuring out who made the call if they traced it there. People from all of the bordering towns funneled into that mall: they'd have a lot of fingerprints to sort through.

Sara Sue picked up the handset... then put it back down. She looked at her purse instinctively, put her hand inside, and fingered the folded pieces of paper with the killer's info on them. She took a deep breath and tried again, picking up the handset but then putting it back down again right away.

She couldn't do it.

For all of her attempts at telling herself otherwise, she *knew* there had been someone outside the day before. It wasn't just the wind blowing tree branches and debris and whatever else Charlie said. Someone had been there. The killer had been outside her house. This guy wasn't going to let up. He wouldn't just forget he had found her and leave her alone. Now that he knew where she lived, he'd be back. Who knew what he'd do the next time? She couldn't just call the cops and think they'd protect her. They couldn't protect her because they wouldn't know who she was if she called from that payphone. But he knew. And that was the one thing she'd always been afraid of.

She had been assuming that calling the cops and getting them involved would mean they would find him soon—like tonight—stopping him from coming back. But what if she didn't have the right information? She had thought about this more than once and still didn't have an answer—at least not one that could calm her nerves. What if the car had been borrowed or stolen? If so, the registration wouldn't be the killer's; it would be some other poor sap's. Should she take the chance that the information was correct? Assume that if she just handed it to the police, they'd find him and lock him up? Or did she keep looking for him on her own?

She knew the answer.

It was the only answer that made sense.

She couldn't sit around waiting, hoping that the cops would find Tina's killer. Even if she handed them all the information she had, it might turn out to be a dead end. And then what? She couldn't stick her head in the sand and hope the guy went away. He was on to her now so he'd be back and he'd do more the next time.

Probably much more.

He couldn't know what she had on him, so he had to assume the worst. Which meant he needed to act fast.

And now so did she.

There was too much at stake for her to sit on her hands. Her life was in danger and so was Charlie's. Anyone close to them might be in trouble too if this guy was that kind of maniac.

As crazy as it sounded, the only way she could be sure they would all be safe is if she found the killer herself.

CHAPTER 43

He had work to do.

The game he had played with Miss Nosy probably scared the hell out of her, but he couldn't leave it at that. She couldn't be allowed to tell the police what she knew, whatever that was. No matter how many times he had thought about it, replayed the night, walked through every second of it, he couldn't think of anything he had messed up. But he had to have left some kind of clue behind. How else would she be on to him?

He sighed and turned his chin up far enough so that the back of his head rested on his back. He shut his eyes and let himself feel the anger building inside him. Mistakes were going to get him caught. He had to do better or he might as well give himself up.

He didn't want that.

This was what he was born to do.

But what if she wasn't on to him? The thought crossed his mind several times. Maybe it was his old self, his old, boring self, who would never have attempted anything as daring as killing Tina right out in the open the way he had, or killing anyone ever, for that matter—maybe it was that person who was trying to save Miss Nosy. Maybe that guy thought she was attractive and didn't want to have to hurt her. The new him tended to agree on that point, though he would have been surprised if the old him was actually into her. That guy didn't seem to like anyone outside of his type: cheerleader-esque silly girls popping their gum and swiping their long hair out of their faces. The new guy? Well, his tastes were a bit more well-rounded. Maybe that guy didn't approve of what he had done to Tina and didn't want him to do it again.

Maybe that guy wanted this new, improved guy to get caught.

He didn't know, but what he was sure of was that there was no way the old guy was getting a say. There was a reason the new guy was there—a reason he had woken up and taken a look around. The old guy was as boring as everyone else in the world. Bland. Nothing stood out about him. Not his house, which he still shared with his mother, not his car, which wasn't even his, really—just another handout that wasn't even registered under his name, not anything. He was generic, run-of-the-mill; average. There wasn't an authentic bone in his body—for God's sakes, his haircut, the one the old him had thought was so cool, was a chain store barber's attempt at something he copied from a poster on the wall of the shop. The old him had been common in every way imaginable.

That guy was gone.

The new guy, the vibrant, unpredictable one was now in charge, and he'd made some changes—minor ones that hadn't called too much attention. He had changed his hair, given it the edge the old guy was looking for. He had added just a little mousse, tousled it around a bit, and let it do what it did. It looked good. The kind of bad-boy-in-a-good-boy's-body look. Poetic, if ever anything ever was. Too bad he couldn't show the new guy off all the time. People wouldn't understand. He was surrounded by boring, lazy do-nothings who loafed around, shuffling through every day, doing everything the same way they had done it the day before. Just like he used to. It was a wonder that more of them hadn't gotten taken off the face of the earth by people like him, the *new* him. He'd see what he could do about that.

But first he had to deal with Miss Nosy.

He sat in his car near one of the mall entrances. Well, not *his* car. The car was actually his brother's if you wanted to get technical about it. It was a hot car—a black 1990 Mustang with low mileage and a killer sound system. His brother was dead—casualty of war—and his mom hadn't bothered to change the registration. Maybe his mother had left the car in Jared's name because she was sentimental, but that wasn't his excuse—he wasn't that kind of sap. He'd just been too lazy to do it. And not just about that. About a lot of things. The old him worked a dead-end job at a department store, stocking shelves and breaking down boxes all day. No money worth counting came out of it; it was like pocket change. The old him didn't have a pot to piss in. But the new guy would change all that soon. In stages. He had to pace things so no one noticed. Once he was out of his mother's house, things would be easier.

So yeah, for all intents and purposes, the car was his. Dead guys didn't need hot cars.

He let himself get lost in the music that was playing. It was an oldie but goodie—one of the more obscure Nirvana tracks from the 90s that he hadn't heard in a while. He was into retro rock. It was just another one of the things that separated him from the idiots around him. He *got* the music, unlike most people his age. Most of them were into Pop; mindless, beat machine studio music with some tone-deaf moron singing over it. But people didn't care—as long as they could dance to it, they were okay; nobody felt the music like he did; they didn't let it get inside of them and move things around. They didn't understand the lyrics—really let the nuances get into their heads. They just shook their hips and rubbed themselves on each other to whatever beat they could find.

That's where Tina's problem had started, wasn't it? That was part of the reason she was lying cold in the ground now.

He didn't like thinking about Tina much anymore. He hated to admit it, but she had gotten to him, had made him act impulsively. Sure, she had helped him unlock his passion, had helped him start fulfilling the fantasies he had been nursing for years, but now that he had tasted what it was like to kill, to watch someone take their last breath, he wouldn't, he *couldn't* stop. It hadn't happened the way he had wanted it to, though. He had wanted Tina for a different purpose; not as his first victim, though she very well might have turned into that in the end. But if he'd known that was what was going to happen, he would've wanted to plan it, to do it *his* way. Not hers. He hadn't wanted his hand forced the way it was, her foul mouth bringing on the punishment that only he could give. But that was water under the bridge now, wasn't it?

He chuckled.

Maybe Tina had been right after all. Maybe she knew more in death than she had ever known in life. Pushing him the way she had had opened doors to him that he'd only ever daydreamed about. Now he was living his fantasies, becoming the person he had always wanted to be. If she hadn't rejected him the way she had after teasing him so much that his balls throbbed, he might have settled for mediocre—found a girl who would have him, married her, and had a litter of kids. He could have ended up in a neighborhood much like Miss Nosy's in the next ten years. He would have been just like everyone else. The thought of it made him sick to his stomach.

He would never have started living. Never have seen blood spilled by his own hands. That was something he didn't want to think about.

But he didn't have to. Tina had fixed that for him.

He let his mind drift to her. He owed her a little reflection for everything she had given him, after all. Besides, it was always good to remember where you came from—wasn't that the popular saying? It probably hadn't ever been truer than it was right then.

He thought back to that day at the party, but really, it started long before that. He had known Tina in high school, but she hadn't known him. She had thought they met for the first time in college. He let her think they had just met—there was no point in telling her they'd been in school together for four years... he didn't really want her looking back at old yearbook photos to find him. Plus, her knowing that he knew who she was and didn't say anything might have freaked her out. The last thing he had wanted to do was make her uncomfortable. And it was easy to just go with it—after all, he did look a little different. The summer between high school and college had been good to him, adding weight and height to his lanky frame. He didn't even feel like the scrawny pimple-faced kid from high school anymore, so he wasn't really lying...

Whatever. It worked for him.

First semester, he had sat near her in Psych, but not too close. He had let her turn to him, see him, say hello first. It had taken six weeks before she did, but it had finally happened. She had dropped her pencil. She had been twirling it in her hand like she always did. Either she thought that looked intellectual or she had been just plain bored. He had liked to watch her during the lecture, whether she was writing, looking up at the professor like a good little girl, nodding off, or playing games on her cell phone. She had been as intriguing to him then as she'd been in high school.

That day, she'd picked up the pencil and looked up at him. He'd tried to act like he didn't notice her at first. It must have worked because she had smiled and said hello when their eyes met. Then she'd turned away. He wasn't a romantic; he couldn't glean anything from their little exchange. There had been no lingering stare, no longing in her eyes. It had all been over in less than thirty seconds.

But then they had started saying hello to each other before class started.

And saying goodbye after class was over.

They'd started walking out into the hall together chatting about the lecture before going their separate ways—her on the other side of campus and him two buildings over from where they stood. Then they started walking out of the building together. These were hardly dates, but he'd been excited by their little exchanges. Through most of his adolescent life, he had wanted to share the same space as Tina, so walking across campus with her had been a big deal to him. He'd hated that he felt that way, hated that she meant so much to him, but now that, too, was in the past.

They had never progressed much farther than that, even after he had spent two semesters working on it. She had a boyfriend she was trying to be faithful to. And let's face it, he hadn't exactly been her type. He wasn't cool like the people she hung out with; he didn't do the same things off campus. She hadn't been into him, not really.

Whatever.

And he hadn't known if he was really into her if he was being honest about it. She had been a little ditsy, a little flighty. Some people might have said that her lighthearted personality was refreshing, but to him, it made her a little less substantive, less intellectual; she was more of a social butterfly than he had been willing to put up with. Could she have talked intelligently about politics? About science? About technology? Or would their conversations mostly have been centered around pop culture; what country Brad Pitt and Angelina Jolie were going to get their next baby from or what dress some other forgettable actress had worn on the red carpet.

But Tina had been beautiful.

Not stunning, not glamorous, but down-home, girl-next-door-gone-city pretty. He had wanted her, regardless of her shortcomings, and there had been many in his book. She had become someone to conquer in the end, more than a real desire.

So, he had kept trying to win her over.

At first, he'd tried the cool-dude routine, which had been hard because everything she thought was hip, he abhorred. He had gotten a haircut and had moussed it up like some of the guys he saw on campus. She had noticed, liked what she saw. He'd known she would. Girls like her always went for outward appearance over brains. Had that made her common? Yeah, it had, but it hadn't mattered to him.

He still wanted her anyway.

He had taken her to the movies, to dinner at a place just a step above fast food—anything more would have been too fancy—they had even done homework together at the library. He thought he was getting somewhere, but then she'd bring up her boyfriend and the rest of the "date" would go downhill fast. Jonathan this and Jonathan that. She wouldn't shut up about him. Jonathan was like a god to her. He couldn't understand why—the guy wasn't all that. Jonathan wasn't intelligent—at least not by his standards, which, he admitted, were a little high—he wasn't particularly athletic, and he wasn't that good looking. So, what was it? What did Jonathan have that had made Tina go crazy over him? What had kept her with Jonathan, even when a candidate that was clearly better suited for her was standing right there every day and Jonathan was off in another city? She was faithful to Jonathan—at least she said she was—when he was probably screwing every girl he could on campus. So why did she stay with him and ignore the good thing she had right in front of her?

He'd thought about that a lot back then.

He'd compared himself to Jonathan in every way—height, weight, build, dress, sense of humor, earning potential, family— any factor he had been able to think of. Okay, Jonathan's sense of style was better than his; that could be fixed easily. Same with some of the other surface variables he had thought of. But Jonathan couldn't grow intelligence, like the weed he had been known to smoke. He had tried weed once to see what the big deal was, especially after he found out that Jonathan did it too, and wished he hadn't. Now it was his only vice. Well, that and killing. He had vowed never to touch anything like cocaine or heroin because, to his chagrin, he had an addictive personality, as the TV psychologists like to call it. He wouldn't even try X because he needed to be in control at all times. He might use it on Miss Nosy, though, and watch her fade in and out of reality... if they had time.

Jonathan didn't have wit or intelligence, culture, or a real future that he could see, at least nothing more than the dead-end job, house, and 2.5 kids that everyone else had to look forward to. That was fine if you could call that a future. He was on to bigger, better things.

And it's all thanks to you, Tina!

He didn't bother to stop the smile from spreading across his face that time.

He looked at his cell phone, checking the time. He was still good. So, he let his mind drift back to the party, back to the night she had teased him and made him so angry that he had to take her mediocre future from her.

He had met her there like they had planned earlier in class. He wasn't going to go, but she had really wanted to, in lieu of dinner and a movie with him, which had made him angry. *She's one of them,* he had to remind himself. *One of the peons who gets off on the humdrum, the mundane.*

The music had been loud, as expected. He'd been fine with the volume, but what they were playing wasn't fit for his ears. Unintelligible words over a pop/techno beat; music that was supposed to make you want to dance. It didn't have that effect on him. Instead, it made him want to run out of the house screaming. But she had liked it. Obviously.

He had gotten there before she did so he saw her almost as soon as she walked in. That had been a feat in and of itself. The place was crowded, packed with coeds high on boat, a weed and PCP concoction that was popular on campus. It was standing room only; the place had been so stuffed with bodies, he could barely see the floor. Not that anyone there would have thought of sitting down and having a conversation with the person they were with before they went outside and screwed. Because that had probably been what most of those people had ended up doing that night—fucking whoever they were able to pull away from the party long enough. At the time, he couldn't help but hope he and Tina would be doing the same thing.

Maybe.

Who knew?

Tina had been over by a table with a punchbowl and pretzels laid out. Wonderful dinner fare—what a spread. The punch had most certainly been spiked; he could smell the alcohol wafting up from the bowl as soon as he had gotten within inches of it. He waited until she'd had some—by the time he made his way over to her she'd had more than he expected her to have had and she was unsteady on her feet. She'd been swaying to the music, a little off beat but not knowing or caring. Her head bobbed as she moved, enjoying the beat as if it were hypnotic, feeling it the way he felt his music, letting it seep into her soul and move her whatever way it wanted to. Her eyes were closed and her lips were partially open. She was in the zone. He had watched her in rapture, moving a little himself to compliment her. He was too far away for anyone to think they were dancing together, but he knew they were.

Just him and Tina... together.

He started to think he had misjudged her, that maybe she was more like him than he thought.

She opened her eyes and spotted him, waved him over. It had been a pleasant greeting, but the beautiful soul-searching he had seen on her face moments before was gone. The charismatic social butterfly was back and he wished she'd go back to wherever she had been hiding and let the other girl back out to play.

He went to her with a smile on his face—that was what she wanted to see, right? She smiled wider as he got closer to her and had reached her hand out to him. He had taken it; it was hot and clammy. Sticky. He'd had the urge to wash his hands right then; he hated dirty things touching him anywhere, but especially on his hands. That wouldn't have looked right at all, though, and if he wanted Tina, which at that moment, with her tight shirt showing the shape of her small, round breasts, he very much did, he had to act normal. He had told himself that he might even have to drink, or at least hold onto a drink and act like he was, so that no one would think he was some geek masquerading as a cool guy. Would any of those drunk, high morons have had the presence of mind to think that way? Had they even noticed him at all? Probably not, but he had to make sure he was in character all the time. There was no room for mistakes, not even little ones.

"Glad you could make it," she had yelled, trying to talk over the music. "I didn't think you were gonna."

"Why not?" he had asked, matching her volume. God, it had been loud in there.

"Well, this doesn't really seem to be your kind of scene."

She *had* noticed. Was that a good thing or a bad thing?

He had decided to make it a good thing. Maybe play up the deer in the headlights act a little bit and see where it got him.

He had smiled wide, hopefully disarmingly, and said, "Well, yeah. But I wanted to be with you, so here I am."

She had smiled noncommittally, kind of tight-lipped but still pleasant. He'd known that look all too well. It was the look that meant she wanted to reiterate her devotion to her boyfriend right there but hadn't want to be an ass about it. Girls like her were all the same. They liked the attention that other men gave them, let themselves be showered with whatever someone was willing to give, as long as they had a way out. When the water got too hot and the guy wanted a little affection for his time and money, they cried rape or harassment or whatever they could think of to get the guy in trouble. Then they'd do the same thing to another guy, then another, and another. The boyfriend never knew what was happening, if he even existed at all. Either that, or the boyfriend heard that same bullshit story she gave everyone else, only he was expected to bash the guy's face in for touching his girlfriend. Most boyfriends did, and then *they* got in trouble for it. Women controlled men like puppets, and only an ignorant man tried to deny that. Only an idiot fought against it.

So, there he'd been, being led around the room like a dog on a leash, following Tina everywhere she went. And she had liked it. He had walked behind her, acting appropriately sheepish. Some of what she'd said was true, of course; partying wasn't his thing. He was more of a loaner and liked it that way. But not knowing what to do with himself in that situation couldn't have been further from the truth. If he had wanted to play coy, he could have done that. If he had wanted to be a drunken asshole who tore the place up and ruined the party, he could have done that too. If they had really wanted to see something, really wanted to get him going, he could have taken someone out right then and there, killed them right in the middle of the room if he had wanted to. That was bravado talking, and he knew it—he had even known it that night —but still, it felt good to think that way. And in the end, it wasn't even that far from the truth.

Tina had led him to a corner of the room where there were fewer people and most were leaning up against the wall. He'd backed into the corner and watched her as she had pulled away from him, just beyond his reach. She had begun dancing again, swaying to the music, her hips rolling back and forth, back and forth. He had liked that. He had watched her, imagining what that hip shaking might look like if she was naked. When he finally looked up at her face—how long had he been staring at her hips? —she'd been smiling. That time it was a small, sensual play on the lips, not her usual, full-on grin. He liked that. He liked that very much.

"Want to dance, Calvin?" she had asked, raising her voice over the music only a little, her sensual tone getting lost in the din. "Come dance with me."

She had reached for him but he had shied away. With a chuckle that he was particularly proud of because it made him sound vulnerable without sounding like a pansy, he had said, "I don't know how."

She had smiled a little wider but then let her lips open a little, showing just the faintest hint of her teeth. God, she was sexy. He had felt himself reacting to her and she hadn't even touched him. He hated that she could do that to him, could make him lose control that way. But he had loved the feeling she gave him even more. She'd swayed a little more, those hips catching the beat and rocking, rocking, rocking. Then she'd turned around and bent over, just enough for him to see the perfect curve of her behind. She had kept the beat, kept up that rocking, but it was different now because he had a view of her behind that was like nothing he had ever seen before. Sure, he had looked at her body before—every inch of it—but he had never noticed how beautiful her behind was. He'd watched it as she moved, rocking, rocking; he'd felt himself rocking with her, keeping time with the beat. Of course he knew how to dance. He had just told her that he didn't to see what she'd do. He had never expected this in response.

She'd stayed that way, her back turned to him, her hair over one shoulder, her face turned as far as it could go to one side, looking back at him. She had been biting her bottom lip, still rocking that beautiful butt in his direction. He had wanted to touch it. He had thought she wanted him to touch it also. Why else would she have put it in his face like that? He remembered thinking that she wanted him; was certain of it. All of their dates, all of their conversations, everything he'd been working on led them to that point. She wanted to be with him. Once they were together, she would forget about Jonathan because she wouldn't need him anymore. She would see that he was far better for her than Jonathan would ever be, and she would drop him. And it was all thanks to his plan, his carefully crafted plan of getting her. It had worked. He had reeled her in like a fish pulled into a boat by a fisherman's line. Now it was time for him to see what he had caught.

His hand had hovered over her behind for a second before he had placed it on one of her round cheeks. He'd wanted to savor the moment, to not rush things, to caress instead of grip, and that was something he had to remind himself of before touching her. Her behind was firm and soft at the same time. He'd rubbed it quickly —a little too quickly, he admitted in hindsight—and he had let his hand dip between her legs to cop more of a feel. He'd imagined feeling her lips through her pants and underwear, imagined his fingers coming away with a smell, flowers and sweat; musk. The thought had excited him even more. He'd pressed himself against her; he was as hard as a rock. But then she'd stood up quick and he pulled his hand away—whatever was about to happen, he hadn't wanted to be caught with his hand in her crotch. She had spun around like a woman possessed and stared at him, her mouth gaping open. It had been as if they were suspended in time—the music was muffled, the people around him seemed frozen in place. He'd almost been able to hear the blood rushing in his ears. He certainly had felt his erection going away. And that had pissed him off.

Then everything had come crashing back—all sound, all sight —with the feeling of skin against skin.

Slap

His face had stung from the blow but he'd refused to bring a hand up to rub his cheek.

"You son of a bitch," she had yelled before running off, disappearing among the bodies that filled the makeshift dance floor. She was gone before he could even draw another breath.

Calvin had stood there for a minute longer, his anger raging. He'd needed to focus, needed to clear his head. That bitch had just humiliated him in front of a room full of her peers—*his peers*, though most of them had never laid eyes on him before. She had slapped him. For what? For doing what she wanted him to do?

Fucking tease.

He remembered that he hadn't been able to stop himself from

thinking about ways to punish her for being such a goddamned tease. He had gotten hard again just thinking about the prospects.

He'd taken a step in the direction in which she had run off, and a guy, a real slob of a dude, had gotten in his way.

"Hey buddy, you don't want to do that. Why don't you just leave?" he'd said.

Calvin had sized the guy up – 5'9", slight build, potbelly from too many beers, lazy lids from too many drugs.

I could kill this guy before he even blinks, he remembered thinking and this time it was more than just bravado… he had wanted to try it out. He'd wanted to test himself, see if he really had the goods, and the guts, to take the guy on, but he decided against it. Too many people had seen what had happened. More guys might come to help the jerk in front of him. Girls too. He hadn't liked those odds.

Calvin had taken a deep breath and walked, going in the other direction, bumping Mr. Hero as he did so. It was a parting shot; he had to do it. He would have looked like a chump if he hadn't.

Whatever.

Calvin had needed some fresh air anyway. The smell of alcohol and sweat had made him want to puke.

He had made it to the door without incident, but he'd caught a couple of stares. He'd stared right back; he couldn't let them think they were getting to him. They weren't. Not really.

He'd scanned the room, looking for Tina. He had just wanted to see the bitch one more time before leaving, but he couldn't find her. She was probably crying in some other guy's arms, turning him on, making him think he'd get some later.

Watch out sucker! She's playing you too, he'd thought.

Fucking tease.

He'd walked out of the party and slammed the door, but he didn't think many people heard it—the music had been too loud. He had walked to his car thinking of ways to get back at Tina. She had to be punished for what she did. She had to be taught a lesson.

You can't play with a man like that, tease him, make him think you're ready to give it up when you're not. And to embarrass him like that in front of so many people! People he had to see on campus. He remembered being so pissed. He wasn't going to just roll over—she was going to pay for what she did.

Calvin had gotten in his car and slammed that door too. Why not? It had made him feel a little better. He'd turned the ignition and put the car in gear. Before driving off, he had put the fingers that had touched Tina's vagina to his nose.

Sweat, perfume, and musk. Pretty much like he thought it would be.

But it had been more than that, if he was being honest. It had been exquisite. Being with a woman was something he'd always wanted to do, and it was the one thing that had alluded him. He didn't want to pay for it; he was too afraid of what he might get for his ten minutes of ecstasy and $50. He had tried to have sex with his next-door neighbor at the beginning of their eleventh-grade summer, but she didn't want to. He'd gotten angry then but hadn't let her see. He thought maybe he could get her to give it up later in the summer. Calvin had worked on her, but she kept saying no. He backed off, afraid she would tell her father what he was doing and then he would have been in deep trouble.

There hadn't been an opportunity since then.

He had smelled his fingers again, had almost stuck them in his nose to get more of the scent. He'd wanted to lick them but knew he'd only get the taste of his own dirty hand. He wished the real thing was right there so he could get up close and personal with it. He had to get Tina back in a position where she wanted him. He couldn't let her go, not smelling the way she did, not feeling the way she felt. He remembered how soft her behind was, how squeezable. Then Calvin had gotten hard again and he decided he was going to do something about it. Why not? No one would notice. It had been too dark to see and most people had been inside at the party. He remembered unzipping his pants and letting out the beast, as he'd taken to calling his penis. Two girls had walked by the car, heading to the party. Their voices were light and airy; a sexy accompaniment to the memory of Tina's vagina. He had gyrated as he worked, enjoying the sensation and the excitement. It was so bad, so very dirty, but man, was it good. He had shut his eyes, enjoying the danger doing so brought with it, and thought about touching Tina, imagining her bare breast cupped in his hand, her lips parted, her voice calling his name.

It had all been over too soon.

Calvin opened his eyes and saw people coming in and out of the mall. He didn't remember shutting them, and he certainly didn't remember baring himself to the world. He tucked the beast back in his boxers hurriedly and zipped up his jeans, trying to look casual to anyone who might be looking his way.

Stupid.

It was one thing to do it at night when no one could see, but during the day? Calvin banged his hand on the steering wheel.

I'm getting sloppy.

He was breathless—he had been working himself up pretty good and he needed to come down. Calvin had things to do and he couldn't cloud his mind with Tina and sex. At least not yet. There would be time for that later. Maybe a nice little threesome with him, Tina, and Miss Nosy. Calvin was pumped up, the memory not only waking the beast but hyping him up to do some damage just like he had that weekend when he paid Tina back for that stunt she had pulled. She hadn't shown up for lunch with him that day as planned. But he guessed he saw that coming. So, he'd called her to meet. He could have just followed her—he knew she'd be leaving from work to go to the park, but he'd decided to play on her sensitivities and see what she'd do. He apologized during their phone call, sounding properly sad, like he had lost his best friend. She'd still been angry, but at least she was listening. She had said she'd meet him at the park and had actually shown up.

Stupid girl.

Calvin had been there waiting for her. If she hadn't shown up, he'd have gone to her house, so the conversation was inevitable, but the idiot had actually gone to a closed park at night to meet someone who had groped her at a party.

Ridiculous.

Too stupid for words.

Certainly, too stupid for him.

Tina had gotten out of the car angry. She'd actually had the nerve to yell at him.

Does she know what I can do to her? he remembered wondering.

That was almost funny now.

Her voice, the loud shrillness of it, had set him off. So had her posture—leaning in, finger-pointing.

Just who the hell did she think she was? He had to put her in her place.

And he had.

He yelled back.

It had escalated.

The rest was history.

Ahh, the memories.

Calvin turned his attention back to the radio. Nirvana was off and U2 was on, Bono's haunting voice lamenting about a woman being dangerous because they didn't know what they wanted. This was *his* music, soulful and honest, not that watered-down garbage they played on the radio over and over and over again. This was the real shit.

He got out of the car singing the rest of the refrain under his breath, the question in the lyrics striking him as profound.

Who's gonna ride Miss Nosy's wild horses?

Me, baby, he thought as a smile crept onto his lips.

He'd ride Miss Nosy's wild horses hard before she went to sleep for good.

CHAPTER 44

Ice cream always helps, even in life-or-death situations.

Sara Sue walked back into the mall after standing in front of the pay phone for God knew how long, looking like she didn't know how to put the money in. She went to the ice cream stand in the food court and got two scoops of pistachio in a cup. She walked through the mall, window shopping and clearing her mind.

She needed to go home.

She needed to get dinner started, to spruce herself up, to mentally prepare for the future she and Charlie deserved.

She needed to find Tina's killer and she needed to do it soon.

So, she walked and ate, trying to figure out her next move. She slowed down in front of the one place she shouldn't have gone near—the store where Tina had worked.

CHAPTER 45

Calvin had just a few things to pick up at the mall. Some clothes—had to stay on top of the latest style—and some music. He walked by the store where Tina used to work for fun. He stood outside the window a while, watching the girls inside do what they did: straighten the clothes on the racks, ask people if they needed help. There weren't many shoppers yet because it was still early, so the girls were milling around the store, trying to look busy. Tina had been friends with most of the people she worked with. He bet that they were still mourning her. In fact, when one of them got close enough to the window, he noticed a button on her shirt with Tina's face on it. How sweet. How very, very touching. He was almost moved to tears.

He almost laughed out loud. Almost.

What would they do if they knew Tina's killer was standing right there, right outside their store, sharing air with them? Would they faint? Call the police? Rush him and try to claw at his face? All three options were on the table. That would be great fun, wouldn't it? Watching them go through the range of emotions, watching them futilely attempt to punish him for taking their dear, precious friend. He almost wanted to announce his presence just so he could see it all play out. He knew he couldn't, but man, that would be great. He'd have to kill them all afterward, of course... that wouldn't be so bad either.

But that was a fantasy for another day.

After amusing himself in front of Tina's store, Calvin walked toward the parking lot, deciding to put his shopping spree to the side. Work first, play later. He had a little planning to do. He had to prepare for Miss Nos—

He couldn't believe his eyes.

Like a gift, she fell right into his lap!

Miss Nosy was walking up ahead, near one of the other exits to the parking lot. He almost didn't notice her, wouldn't have if he hadn't been looking ahead, through the people in the mall, his mind focused on the more pressing matter of planning out how he'd kill, well, her.

As she was leaving the mall, Calvin saw her smile at a woman who was on her way into the mall using the same door. Before going through the second set of glass doors, Miss Nosy threw out a container from the ice cream store. She looked like she didn't have a care in the world—like it was just a normal day.

That really pissed him off.

Calvin wanted a closer look.

He jogged toward her, being careful not to look suspicious; he was just a guy in a hurry. He exited the glass doors in time to see her walk into the parking lot. He moved quickly covering the ground between them fast, but then slowed to a normal pace as he approached her. It took everything he had to regulate his breathing and maintain a normal gait after running the way he had but he did it. He walked right past her... and she didn't even so much as glance in his direction.

Calvin snickered under his breath at how clueless she was. How absolutely oblivious.

She looked for her car, her eyes turning in his direction but never landing on him, never registering recognition.

See anything familiar? he thought.

No?

Too bad for you babe.

Look at Miss Nosy, hanging out in the mall. Strolling. Shopping. Acting like all was right with the world. Maybe she wasn't all that scared after all.

But she would be.

She'd underestimated Calvin, thought he was a joke. That was a mistake. A huge one.

He'd have to do something about that, wouldn't he? He'd have to make sure she respected him, feared him, the way she should. It would be a lesson she'd never forget.

Calvin smiled, shook his head absently for the audience, should he have one, and went back into the mall, hurrying to an athletic store like that had been his destination all the time. He needed to kill time, needed to let her leave the mall before he went to his parking lot entrance and got into his car. He actually tried on a pair of shoes, thought about buying them. He was in no rush. There was no need to follow her. He knew the way to her house.

CHAPTER 46

Sara Sue.

She had been on his mind all day.

When she answered her cell phone, she sounded fine—better than fine, really. She sounded like her old self; the Sara Sue he married, the one he fell in love with, the one who had disappeared for a while. A long while. He was happy to have her back, was genuinely excited that she seemed to have resurfaced, but it also worried him a little. What had changed? She had been terrified yesterday, afraid of her own shadow, and today everything was all sunshine and roses? Maybe last night was the breaking point and this was all over. Wishful thinking, but what a wonderful thought it was. Could he really go home and be normal, not mention yesterday, and just see what happened? Maybe. Maybe that was *exactly* what he should do. In fact, that was what he was leaning toward. He'd go get some flowers, have a nice dinner—go back in time, do the things they used to do... the things they used to enjoy. Charlie welcomed it; it had been too long since they'd had real fun together. Maybe they could do something together—nothing fancy, just dinner and a movie, a little snuggling, a little kissing, maybe a little action. They deserved it. He felt guilty that it was coming on the back of that woman's death, but he'd deal with that later.

If Sara Sue was in a good mood, let her be in a good mood. If she brought up what happened, he'd be there to help her. If not, he wouldn't bring it up either.

It sounded a lot like avoidance, but Charlie didn't want to psychoanalyze himself.

He just wanted things to go back to normal. He wanted his wife to be his wife and not some lesbian murderer. He just wanted Sara Sue back.

If only for one night.

Because Charlie knew they couldn't avoid the issue forever. What if someone else knew what Sara Sue had done? They might be planning to tell the police, might be thinking of blackmailing her. He couldn't let that happen. They had to form an ironclad alibi, and they could only do that together. So, they would have to talk about it, and soon... it just didn't have to be today.

He left the shop early; thankful he'd been able to finish the cars in his queue before lunch. He was on a mission. First, he'd get some flowers, then he'd head home, take some steaks out to throw on the grill later. They could have a nice evening together like they used to, just relaxing on the deck, feeling the late-day sun on their faces.

Real life could wait.

CHAPTER 47

Calvin slid in behind a pair of parked cars and turned off the engine. He was three doors away from Miss Nosy's house. She wasn't home yet—he'd checked. He had looked in the windows on the garage doors—one of the stupidest creations known to man, in his opinion. They made it far too easy for someone to see if anyone was home. There were a lot of little things that people did that just didn't make any sense, and putting windows in their garage doors was one of them.

He had been prepared to ring the doorbell and push her back inside when she answered because why not add forced entry to his repertoire? The neighbor across the street seemed to have her hands full with kids—he had looked in on her too, just to be sure—and the street seemed otherwise deserted, but that may not happen now. It was the middle of the day, and while it looked like everyone was out working, and he'd only be outside her door for thirty seconds at the most, he'd still have to check for peeping eyes again, and modify his plan if necessary.

Miss Nosy was *always* making him modify his plans.

Now that he was stuck waiting, he thought up a couple of ways to make Miss Nosy's acquaintance.

Calvin was driving his car today, not a rental. It was a risk he hadn't meant to take, but he had acted on impulse and driven to her place after seeing her at the mall. It was a mistake he hoped didn't come back to bite him. He needed to be as incognito as possible.

So, she hadn't gone right home after the mall like he thought she would. Out gallivanting, huh? Neither had he. He had made a stop at the hardware store on the way to buy a couple things for her, some things she really wouldn't like. He wanted to have fun with Miss Nosy, show her the time of her life. Take her breath away figuratively, and then do it for real.

He had a couple hours to kill before the hubby came home.

Talk about serendipity? She had been on his mind constantly. His fantasies were now all about Miss Nosy, crowding out his usual fare. He wanted to see how she would look when she saw the beast. That would be the first thing he'd show her, let her get a good look. Then he'd show her the knife. Would she like the beast? Of course she would. But she wouldn't like the knife. Not one bit.

Poor Miss Nosy. She really didn't know what was in store for her.

Calvin was anxious to get the show on the road but had to stay calm. It would happen soon enough. He slid down in his seat and settled in. He might be waiting a while. He hoped not. He was ready, so very ready; his body was almost thrumming with anticipation. But good things come to those who wait.

CHAPTER 48

Sara Sue headed for Falls Junction after leaving the mall.

It took her a while to decide to do it—partly because she was uncertain about what to do next, partly because she was afraid—but once she made up her mind, there was no stopping her. When she got in the car, she pulled out the original list of tasks and the address she had gotten from the auditor's office—the very information she had been prepared to burn just a few hours before. Sara Sue used her phone to get directions to his house from the mall. She reviewed the list again, refreshing her memory, making a plan.

Like it or not, she was back on the case.

1. *Tina was from Falls Junction*—check.

Somewhere along the line she'd added a question about her lifestyle. Sara Sue could barely make out her chicken scratch looping along the side of the paper, tiny and tight as she started to run out of space.

Was she a hard partier? That's what the scrawled notes amounted to, and so far, Sara Sue hadn't seen anything that pointed to that being true. She seemed to be the same as other folks her age. No obvious drug use. She didn't seem to be part of a bad crowd.

2.*Tina had a boyfriend who goes to college in DC*—Jonathan.

He would have been her fiancé if he'd had the chance to pop the question. Sara Sue didn't think he was the killer anymore. That was real emotion he'd shown at the funeral. Unless he was an incredible actor, he had nothing to do with Tina's murder.

3.*There was a MySpace tribute up about Tina.*

Been there. She hadn't gotten anything from the tribute page. No proclamations, no weird posts. Just sad people missing their friend.

4.*Have license plate number.*

That had expanded into her finding the address she had called up directions to on her phone. Sara Sue added a note to this point: *Have a name and address but what if they aren't right? What if the car was stolen?*

That was the end. She turned the paper over in her hand, noting the hastily written secondary lists—the daily tasks that were supposed to help her answer the questions on the main list, but didn't find anything she needed to address. The list felt unfinished somehow; like it was missing something, just like a dish missing an ingredient. Sara Sue had covered a lot of the bases, but not all of them. She was missing *something*, and she had a feeling it was big.

And then it came to her with painful clarity.

In perfect print, she added the one thing she couldn't afford to forget.

5.*He knows I know.*

As Sara Sue drove to Falls Junction, she wondered what she expected to find. His house would probably look normal, just like the other houses on the street. There wouldn't be some calling card, some glaring sign with neon paint that read, "You found me! I'm the killer!" So, what did she think she'd see?

And what did she plan to do once she got there? Ring the doorbell and say hello? Tell him she knew he was outside her house trying to scare her and that she knew what he did to Tina? Ask him to please turn himself in because it was the right thing to do?

She needed a better plan than just showing up. But she didn't have one. And she was almost there.

The one time she wanted the directions to be wrong just to give her a little more time to come up with a plan, they were dead on. She got to the house within five minutes of getting off the highway.

It was a regular house—a red brick rambler probably built in the 1950s. It had a picture window in the front room and sat on a nice plot of land. It had a long driveway leading up a slight incline.

Sara Sue confirmed the address with the output from the auditor's office and the number on the doorframe, big black digits against a white door casing fashioned to look like the detail on a Greek pillar.

They matched.

So, this was where Tina's killer lived.

Jared Corning.

Sara Sue stared at the house from her not-so-hidden hiding place across the street and two houses down. She looked around at the houses nearby, surveyed the middle-class neighborhood with big, old trees and sidewalks. She imagined kids playing there, riding their bikes and drawing hopscotch grids. Did he watch them? Had he ever hurt one of them?

Five minutes turned into ten.

No one came in or out of the house.

The lawn was well manicured and speckled with annuals around the front and sides. He liked to garden. Or did he live with someone—a woman? Was she his wife? His girlfriend? Sara Sue looked around again. It was an old neighborhood. Not the kind a young couple would move into unless they had to. Did he live with his mother? Did Tina's killer—the big, bad bastard who liked bashing girls' heads in—live with his Mommy? The thought made Sara Sue laugh. Maybe he wasn't so tough after all.

Five more minutes and still nothing.

What was she waiting for anyway? She felt stupid sitting there. Sara Sue had no plan, no idea of what her next move should be. If someone walked out of the house and up to the car, she didn't even know what she would say.

Sara Sue decided to leave before she got herself into trouble.

She needed to think out a game plan before doing anything else. It had been stupid to go there without one and she was lucky no one was there to see her. She was acting on impulse, just doing whatever felt right, and that was going to get her killed.

Sara Sue drove back to her neck of the woods, stopped at the supermarket and picked up a couple of things for her Mars rendezvous, thinking all the while of what her next step would be on the case. Now she knew where *he* lived; that leveled the playing field a little. As long as the registration was right that was, which was a huge assumption to make. One she was afraid to bank on.

CHAPTER 49

He was still there.

Charlie was parked at the end of his own street. He'd stopped there when he saw a man walk from his driveway and get into a black Mustang. Charlie had pulled over, hoping to catch a glimpse of the guy's face when he drove by, but he'd never left. He just got in his car, and there he sat. So, Charlie sat. Now they had both been sitting there for over ten minutes.

Who the hell was this guy? A salesman? Did anybody really do door-to-door sales anymore? Charlie doubted it. Anyway, this guy didn't look like a salesperson; he looked more like a college boy. So why was a college boy waiting for his wife to get home?

Had he been wrong? Maybe Sara Sue didn't have anything to do with the murder. Maybe this guy, this *kid*, was her lover and not Tina. Maybe she was late for their afternoon romp and he was waiting outside for her like a good little puppy.

Charlie was starting to get mad. His mind didn't let up on the possibilities.

Maybe he was right about Sara Sue and Tina being together;

that would still explain how she knew Tina in the first place. But maybe the guy was a third person in the equation. A love triangle. Were the three of them lovers? Or had Sara Sue stolen Tina from this guy?

There were too many questions, too many scenarios. He was driving himself crazy.

Charlie put the car in gear and got ready to pull out from behind the Toyota his neighbor parked on the street. He was going to approach the guy like a man and demand to know what he was doing in front of his house. If he was sleeping with Sara Sue, he better be man enough to own up to it, or Charlie planned to beat it out of him. Enough was enough. There was but so much a man could take. Someone waiting outside his house for a booty call with his wife was Charlie's final straw.

Charlie cut the wheel, about to give his car some gas. He almost pulled out in front of the car coming up his street.

But she didn't notice.

Sara Sue drove right by him, oblivious to Charlie. He watched the back of her head as she passed the guy's car too; she didn't even look at it. Maybe that was part of the plan; she was just supposed to drive home like she didn't know he was there and then he'd approach the house. Or maybe she didn't see him because she had other things on her mind, like what position she planned to screw him in this time.

Charlie was royally pissed off now, beside himself with anger.

He gripped the steering wheel so hard, his knuckles turned white. He wanted to speed up behind her, trap the car in the driveway, break up their little tryst, but he forced himself to sit still, to wait, to watch. If he was going to find out what was really going on, he'd have to sneak up on them. He might still beat the guy up —Charlie really wanted to feel the guy's cheek collapse under his fist—but not at the expense of getting the proof he needed... the proof she couldn't deny.

He wanted to know what was going on, right? Well, there was

no time like the present. Sara Sue would have no opportunity to lie when everything was laid bare. Charlie shook his head, furious with the situation, with Sara Sue, and with himself. He couldn't believe he had wanted to *help* her. What a joke. He felt like an idiot again, like some stupid lackey following behind Sara Sue, the super bitch. He was willing to let the affair with Tina go, was willing to help her cover up a murder, for God's sake! But now there was another lover? Some little boy barely out of his teenage years? What the hell was that?

He felt manipulated, tricked.

He felt played.

Charlie loosened his grip on the steering wheel and sat back in his seat, getting more and more comfortable with his plan. He'd wait until the guy made it into the house before approaching on foot. He'd let himself in and probably catch them half out of their underwear. If Charlie played his cards right, he could beat the hell out of the guy before he had time to pull his pants up.

CHAPTER 50

Sara Sue bounded up the stairs to the front door with a new spring in her step. So much to do, so little time. She needed to figure out her next move with the killer; she couldn't afford to waste any time. She also needed to get dinner started and set the mood before Charlie got home if she wanted to have a nice evening with him. She wasn't going for anything fancy, just comfy. She was leaving the fancy stuff for Mars day, which she still needed to plan. So, what should she do first, catch a killer or cook dinner?

Dinner won.

She started on the grill—Charlie teased her because it always took Sara Sue forever to get the coals going—and set the table. Charlie loved to eat outside, so that's what they'd do. The afternoon was beautiful; the sun was gorgeous and the light breeze whistling through the trees would keep them cool.

It would be perfect.

She came back into the kitchen and started washing the lettuce for a salad and sautéing garlic while she thought about her next move with the killer. The guy knew where she lived, that much she was aware of. He had probably been at the funeral or at the cemetery and spotted her there. Maybe he had known everyone else at the funeral and she had stuck out like a sore thumb. Maybe he saw her the night of the murder and had just been biding his time, toying with her. God, that was a scary thought. What if he'd been watching her, waiting outside in the woods, this whole time? He could have gotten her so many times, snatched her out of her house and taken her God knew where. What was he waiting for? She looked out the window above the sink, surveying her back-yard, suddenly terrified again. She wondered whether he was out there right then, watching, waiting, laughing at how frightened he was making her. He probably liked it, the fear showing on her face. She remembered the way he stood over Tina; he seemed to soak up her pain.

He's sick, she thought.

Probably completely delusional. She wouldn't be able to talk her way out of it if he came for her.

Sara Sue looked away from the window and pulled the blinds, taking away the beautiful sunshine that filled the room and replacing it with muted light. She needed to think, not be afraid of her own shadow. Coming up with things he might be doing right then wasn't going to help. Next, she would be thinking of what method he'd use to kill her, and what good would that do?

But her mind took that flash of an idea and ran with it, pulling away even as she tried to grab at it and wrangle it back into submission. Would he use a gun or a knife on her? Would he torture her in the privacy of her own home, do all sorts of obscene things to her? He would come early—before Charlie got home from work. He wouldn't want to risk a confrontation with someone his own size. Maybe he couldn't handle himself with guys. Could that work to her benefit?

She glanced at the clock; it was 3:15.

He would come early enough to do his business and get away without rushing... like now.

The smell of burning garlic was thick in the air, but she didn't stop to turn on the vent or move the pan off the burner. She raced into the front room to check the front door.

It was locked.

She checked the door leading to the garage—it was locked too.

She ran through the house checking the locks on the windows —they were all engaged.

The smoke alarm was going off. The high-pitched beeping was loud enough to drive her crazy.

She went back to the kitchen, glancing over at the alarm keypad mounted on the wall next to the front door. The alarm wasn't on. She had protested getting the alarm when they moved in; she didn't want to feel like a prisoner in her own home or like Big Brother was watching. Until she spent her first night home alone. After that, she had been thankful to have it, to know that the police were only a few minutes away. She needed that sense of security now. Sara Sue took a step toward the alarm but changed directions abruptly. The pan was going to catch on fire if she didn't get it off the burner soon. The smoke alarm was going to drive her absolutely batty if she didn't make it stop. She turned toward the kitchen and noticed how much light was still in the house. She had closed every other blind except the glass door to the deck. She walked over to it, ignoring the wailing alarm. This was more important... as long as the house didn't burn down. But before she reached the door, a shadow blocked the sun.

She looked up, her eyes adjusting to the different light. She didn't recognize the man standing there, but she didn't need to. His expression said it all. The smile that played on his lips was malicious, evil, the kind you'd expect to see on a vampire. His eyes were cold and hard.

It was Tina's killer.

They stared at each other, only a thin plate of glass between them. Sara Sue was glued in place, frozen with fear. He was enjoying himself, playing out the scene as though it was part of a movie script. He was on the deck, shielded from view from either side of the house because of the trees on one side and the gazebo on the other. And there were just woods behind the house, beautiful, lush trees that she loved to watch go through their cycles—leaves turning color then falling away only to sprout anew... gorgeous trees that would hide her murder from anyone who might have seen. It was the perfect set up and he knew it. It was just her and him.

Again.

His smile changed a little, became a little smaller, a little more sinister. Her heart jumped in her chest. Slowly, soundlessly, he was opening the glass door, sliding it back while they stared at each other.

She jumped, literally leapt into motion, and ran across the room and down the steps toward the front door. She passed by her purse along the way—it was sitting on the sofa—but she couldn't turn around to get it. There was no time. He would be inside any second, if he wasn't already, and she only had one chance to get out of the house.

Sara Sue fingered the lock and it kept slipping out of her grasp. It was like in the movies when people couldn't seem to get away from the slow-walking supernatural baddie no matter how fast they ran. It was as if she had oil on her hands; she couldn't keep a decent enough grip on the lock to turn it.

Sara Sue could almost feel his breath on her neck.

She shrieked despite herself, tears burning at the corners of her eyes. She couldn't help but think that this was it. This was the way she was going to die. He'd come in; do whatever he wanted with her, and then he'd kill her, leaving a bloody mess for Charlie to find. How would Charlie ever recover from that?

But there was no time to think about what could be. If she fooled around too long, it *would* be. She gave the lock one last try. It was all she had time for; she could hear him shutting the sliding door...wouldn't want people to hear her screaming, right? If she couldn't get a grip on the lock this time, it was all over. There wasn't that much ground to cover between the deck door and the front door. Her heart pounded in her chest as she imagined his footsteps behind her.

She grabbed the lock and turned it. Without hesitation, she whipped the door open... and saw Charlie standing there with his key out. He looked angry, very angry, and a little surprised. She didn't have time to waste worrying about Charlie's facial expressions. They needed to get out of there if they were going to make it through this. She pushed at him but it was like hitting a brick wall.

Charlie was looking over her shoulder. Did he see him? He had to. The guy was right on her tail. What the hell was he doing? They needed to run.

"Come on!" Sara Sue shouted and tried to push Charlie out of the doorway, but he didn't budge. In fact, he pushed her back inside. She couldn't stop him no matter how hard she tried.

"Charlie—," she began, but he cut her off.

"What's your hurry, babe?" he said in the coldest voice she'd ever heard him use. His eyes bore into her, cutting like knives. "We don't want to be rude to your guest."

"Wha—" she started as she turned around, but the words got caught in her throat. The killer was close. Very close.

Charlie and Sara Sue saw the knife at the same time.

Charlie shouted something unintelligible, shoved her out of the way, and lunged up the stairs toward Tina's killer. Sara Sue fell against the wall and slid to the floor before she could stop herself, momentum had her flopping around bonelessly, like a rag doll.

She stood up and tried to find a way into the fight.

Charlie and Tina's killer had crashed into an end table and knocked over the lamp by the time Sara Sue got up the few stairs that led to from the front door to the living area. She got there just in time to see them flip over the back of the sofa and fall onto the floor. Charlie was on top, but not for long. They jockeyed for position, rolling as far as the living room furniture would let them. Charlie was keeping the knife at bay and trying to punch the guy with his free hand. The killer, considerably younger, but not quite as strong as Charlie, was throwing his weight behind the arm holding the knife, trying to drive it into Charlie's chest, neck—wherever he could reach. He had youth on his side. Charlie had brawn.

Sara Sue needed to do something. She couldn't hit the guy with anything because she might hit Charlie instead. They were moving so erratically that she didn't think she could get a clean shot anyway. Charlie and the murderer were fighting so violently, she was afraid to jump in but she had to. Tina's killer had a knife. Her husband needed her help.

She opened her cell phone, put it on speaker, and called 911, all the while looking for a chance to jump into the fray. She dropped the phone on the sofa as she sized up the fight, trying to figure out a way to get an arm around the killer's neck. Sara Sue hoped the dispatcher could hear her, but there was no time to think about that now. The guy still had the knife in his hand and Charlie was getting tired.

Sara Sue shouted their address to the dispatcher and told them someone was trying to kill them. She hoped they heard her. Their lives depended on it.

Charlie got the upper hand and jumped to his feet fast. He tried to kick Tina's killer before he could get up too, but he missed and almost fell.

Tina's killer stood up with a quickness they didn't anticipate and lunged at Charlie, trying to take advantage of the miss, but it didn't work. Charlie caught him by the arm, spun him around, and held him out far enough to throw a right cross without letting go of the arm he held with his left. And then another. Then Sara Sue saw her chance. She got behind them and looped her arm around the killer's neck and squeezed, pulling him down, arching his back painfully.

"Get out of this, Sara Sue!" Charlie yelled. "Call the police!"

"I did. They're on their way!" She hoped that was the truth.

"Get away from him!" Charlie said, breathlessly.

That was not good.

She wanted to say, "I'm not leaving you," but she didn't get the chance. Tina's killer hit Sara Sue in the ribs with his elbow. It hurt like hell, but she was too afraid to let go. He'd kill them for sure if he got the upper hand again. He'd take Charlie first because he was the biggest threat. And Charlie was winded; he hadn't had this much activity in years. Charlie was tired, and if she could see it, so could this bastard. He'd probably knock her out and tie her up so that if she woke up while he was killing Charlie, she couldn't do anything about it. Then once he got done with Charlie, he'd work on her. The police wouldn't get there in time to save them.

Sara Sue held on to his neck for dear life, even as tears rolled down her cheeks and her breath came in short bursts, clipped from the pain in her ribs.

Charlie rushed him again.

The guy swiped at him with the knife but missed. The knife was a scary looking Swiss Army deal. Dangerous but small. She and Charlie thought the same thing at the same time. She let go of his neck and they both grabbed his arm—four hands suddenly pushing down one—and pinned him to the floor. He kicked and grunted, calling Sara Sue all sorts of bitches and he threw out a slew of other threats, but it was futile. They had him.

And he knew it.

Sara Sue was panting, gasping for air.

So was Charlie.

It took everything they had to keep the killer down. Sara Sue damn near laid down on him to keep his other arm out of the way, pinning it down with her body, and Charlie kneed the killer in the ribs. Sara Sue clawed at his face when she could get to it; it felt good to rip at his skin and see blood.

She heard something outside. It added to the din—the obscene mix of panting, grunting, and the incessant blaring of the fire alarm.

Something was coming.

Something loud.

A fire engine in the distance.

The calvary! At least a part of it. They needed people with guns, but at that point any help would do. As long as they could keep the guy restrained. She didn't know how much longer she and Charlie could do it themselves.

It was then that she noticed the smoke filling the room and the horrible smell of burning. She could see sparks of light coming from the kitchen.

Fire.

The garlic, the pan, everything had caught on fire. She'd never thought she would say this about something that could have burned her house down but *thank God*.

The fire alarm had not only started blaring in the house, but it had triggered an alert to the alarm company. They had dispatched the fire engine so that theirs and every house on the block didn't succumb to the flames. They had probably called her while she was on the phone with the 911 operator. Sara Sue didn't know— she had been otherwise occupied.

Charlie and his monitors and alarms.

Bless him.

Bless the firefighters.

Bless them all.

"It's a fi—," she wanted to state obvious. Surely Charlie had heard it himself, but she was just so happy that help was on its way she couldn't hold it in. But she didn't get the chance to finish. Tina's killer had twisted under her while her body relaxed, relief washing over her as the fire engine approached. He leaned up, twisted his neck to an impossible angle, and bit her on the cheek. The pain was like nothing she'd ever experienced before. She could feel her blood wetting her face in torrents. She could feel air hitting the soft flesh beneath the epidermis, stinging it. It felt like he had bitten her deep enough that her teeth and gums would be visible through the holes he had surely left. Sara Sue yelped and pressed her hands to her face, leaving Charlie to deal with Tina's killer alone before realizing what she had done. It had been instinct. And it had been a mistake.

Tina's killer had caught a second wind lying there on his back. She had been so elated to hear the fire engine that she hadn't noticed that the killer wasn't fighting as hard anymore. He rolled over fast and hit Charlie on the back of his head with his free hand, clubbing him. Charlie went down hard. Sara Sue screamed for him, but it was no use. He was out cold.

She stood up and backed away. Now Tina's killer had the upper hand.

"You little bitch," he said. His mouth sounded like it was full of marbles and was a bloody mess. Maybe Charlie had knocked a couple teeth out.

It wasn't slowing him down.

Sara Sue felt a chill wash over her body as he looked her up and down. He laughed—it sounded low and guttural, and it was the most terrifying sound she had ever heard. "You and your husband think you can fight *me*?"

"I know what you did. I know who you are."

It just came out; she was saying it before she knew her lips were moving.

He laughed and blood sprayed out of his mouth and onto the sofa—the *cream* sofa.

That's not gonna come out, she thought.

"You know what I did?" he said mockingly. "Tell me. What did I do?"

He was walking toward Sara Sue, backing her against a wall.

"You killed Tina. You smashed her face in with a rock."

"Yeah? And how do you know that?"

"I-I was there. I saw you do it."

Should she be saying these things? Telling him everything like this? Maybe not, but she had to do something. If she could keep him talking, maybe Charlie would wake up and help her fight him again. Maybe she could buy enough time for the firefighters to get into the house and help—that axe they used would do nicely. If she kept him talking, maybe she could get out of this somehow. If not, they were dead. Either this bastard was going to kill them or the fire would take them all.

She suppressed a cough as the smoke started to fill the room.

The nasty smile that had returned to his face faltered a bit.

"You couldn't have seen that, you idiot. You don't know what you're talking about."

He was nervous.

Maybe that was a good thing.

He coughed too; the smoke was getting to him. It was catching up to Sara Sue pretty quickly—combined with the pain from her ribs she was nearly gasping for air—but she was afraid to duck down. She wouldn't have enough mobility on the floor. She'd be too easy to catch.

"I did see you," she continued. "I was at the top of the hill in my car. I watched the whole thing happen." Sara Sue hesitated, unsure if she should go on. But she had to. She was talking to save their lives. "I saw you kill her, Jared."

His face genuinely brightened as he laughed out loud.

"Jared? Is that who you think I am? Oh, Miss Nosy, you got it all wrong. But nice try. You certainly have been a busy little bee to come up with that name."

Shit.

All of this and she still had the wrong guy. She and Charlie were going to die for nothing. They were going to die because she was a nosy, inconsiderate bitch.

Charlie groaned on the floor.

Sara Sue heard and wished she hadn't. He was too late to help her fight, but just in time to see her die.

Tina's killer heard it too and stopped walking toward her. He looked over at Charlie and saw that he was moving a little, coming out of it.

"Let me take care of this little inconvenience first, sweetheart, and then we'll start *our* date."

He took a step toward Charlie before turning back to her, his voice disarming, almost pleasant.

"Don't go anywhere."

CHAPTER 51

I had it all wrong.

That's all Charlie could think as he lay there listening to Sara Sue and that bastard talking. This wasn't some act they were putting on to throw him off; Sara Sue's fear was real. Her voice was quavering—he thought she must have been shaking like a leaf. The beating she'd let loose on the man was real too—she hadn't been pulling any punches. None of this was for effect. He had misjudged his wife in a big way.

He felt sick. Five minutes before, he had been trying to walk in on Sara Sue with her lover and... well, he really didn't know what he had planned to do once he saw them. He would have fought the guy, no doubt about it. He would have wanted to call it quits with Sara Sue but would he have? *Could* he have left her? He didn't know the answer to that question and that frightened him a bit.

But there was no time to think about that right now.

The guy who killed Tina was taunting Sara Sue, backing her up slowly, making her feel like a trapped animal. She would fight hard before she died, Charlie knew that. Sara Sue wouldn't just roll over —she would fight until she couldn't anymore; she would make sure to take a piece of him with her. But fight or no fight, she would die. That bastard had a weapon and Sara Sue didn't.

Charlie fought to sit up, but he was so dizzy he could hardly see. He had to fight through it. He had to get it together or they were both dead.

His wife needed him.

She always had.

Charlie let out a moan. It sounded a bit theatrical to his ears, but he hoped the guy didn't see through it. He needed to lure him away from Sara Sue so he could make one last ditch effort at subduing him for the cops.

He coughed—that was real.

If Charlie couldn't subdue him, maybe the diversion would be long enough for Sara Sue to make a run for it.

CHAPTER 52

It was *not* supposed to happen this way!

Calvin was frantic inside but he had to maintain his cool veneer. If he showed even a modicum of fear, Miss Nosy might try to attack him from behind. He needed to control her and hoped his attitude would be enough. But she was strong, tough. Taking care of her wouldn't be as easy as he thought it would be.

And then there was the question of the guy.

He was obviously her husband—they were wearing matching wedding bands. And he was strong as hell. It was dumb luck that Calvin had been able to hit him on the back of his head hard enough to knock him out. The guy easily outweighed him by fifty pounds. And he was motivated.

What the hell was he doing home so early? He should still be at work like the rest of the people in their shitty little neighborhood. Calvin had banked on having some time with Miss Nosy; he had some things he had wanted to show her. But he had gotten less than five minutes alone with her.

Stupid.

He hadn't watched them, hadn't taken the time to learn their patterns.

He had been impulsive again.

Emotional.

Amateurish.

And this time it might get him killed.

This thing had turned to shit before he could blink an eye.

Calvin wished he could leave and try it again another day. Or just forget the whole thing and let the little bitch live. But it was too late for that. They had both seen him and would definitely tell the police. She had gotten closer than she knew, finding out his brother's name. It wouldn't have taken much to figure out that Jared was dead and that he was driving the car. Everybody knew Calvin had it, they even ridiculed him for it, said he was a wannabe. Calvin knew it was really because they were jealous and he didn't care what they thought anyway. There wasn't anyone he could ask to lie for him, except maybe his mother, and he wouldn't ask her to help him—*couldn't*. She didn't need to be involved in any of what was going on, didn't need to hear anything about what he did when she wasn't looking.

Calvin had to kill them.

There was no turning back now.

The fire was getting worse; the heat and smoke were really working on him. His eyes burned; his throat felt raw. He was starting to cough. Soon the coughing would get the better of him and he'd be unable to do anything but that. He needed to get them into another room, kill them, then get hell out of there. If he didn't hurry, the fire would get all of them.

Then there was the issue of the fire engine pulling up. They were right around the corner if he was guessing correctly. He had less than a minute to make a move.

Can't kill them both.

Calvin walked over to Miss Nosy's husband, trying to display a confidence he didn't feel. There was enough time to kill one of them, and it might as well be him. He'd grab Miss Nosy and leave the house before the fire engine parked, leaving her husband bleeding to death on the floor, his lungs filling with smoke. If he cut him in the right place, across the jugular, there was no chance he'd survive.

You only get one shot at this, Calvin, he hissed at himself. *Do it right.*

CHAPTER 53

Sara Sue let the killer think she was going to sit idly by while he slaughtered her husband. She let him think she was so afraid she couldn't move. But she was past immobility now and fear couldn't describe what she felt. She was in fight or flight mode and she had chosen to fight. And the fact was, he was probably going to kill them both anyway.

She had nothing to lose.

In her excitement she had thought the fire engine was much closer, but still, they should have been there by now. She was pretty sure the killer still had enough time to kill one of them if he really wanted to, and it looked like he indeed wanted to. He had picked Charlie. She couldn't let that happen. Even if it meant her own life.

The killer turned his back on Sara Sue and walked toward Charlie.

One step.

Two steps.

On his third step, Sara Sue picked up the lamp that had been knocked over during the fight. It was broken; big ceramic pieces jutted out like teeth.

Four steps.

Five steps.

She had a good grip on the broken lamp, its jagged side pointing down. She had to hit him right or it wasn't going to work. If she didn't do it hard enough, it would just make him angry.

Six steps.

She moved quickly—faster than she ever had—and got right behind him with the lamp cocked out to the side. She hit him in the temple before he could take his seventh step.

The ceramic dug into the side of his head just like she hoped it would.

Tina's killer wobbled on his feet as the blood started to pour from his temple. He dropped his knife, but his arm remained suspended in air as if he was still holding it. He never turned back around to face her, and that was a shame; she would have liked to watch him die. Instead Charlie, who had sat up after Sara Sue swung the lamp, got the view.

The killer dropped to his knees and stayed there for a moment, his neck losing strength; his head dropping to one side. He tried to lift it but couldn't. He fell to the floor with a groan, hitting his face on the hardwood with a loud crack. He probably broke his nose. She didn't think it mattered anymore.

Somebody was in the driveway, about to come up to the door. Firefighters? The police? Probably both.

She looked over at her purse, took a mental inventory of everything that was in there that could incriminate her and moved fast. She stepped over Tina's killer and grabbed her purse off the sofa, all the while terrified that he was going to grab her leg like they always did in the movies. She cast a quick glance at him before running toward the kitchen: his face was flat on the floor, nose mashed against it with blood pooling under his mouth and from the wound to his temple.

He was dead for sure.

At least she hoped.

The fire was hot, especially as close as she was standing. But she had to make it look realistic. She threw her purse into the room, hoping it landed about midway, right in the heart of the fire. She didn't even take a second to breathe before rushing over to Charlie who was kneeling over Tina's killer, checking for a pulse.

He shook his head.

Her heart felt lighter than it had in days.

"He's dead, baby. You saved us."

Sara Sue was so relieved to hear those words that she almost cried. They knelt on the floor where the air wasn't as bad yet and crawled toward the front door.

Bang.

The cavalry was coming in.

Finally.

Bang.

One more loud bang and the front door busted in, reduced to splinters. Firefighters ran in, grabbed them under the arms, and yanked them out of the house. Police waited for the okay then entered the house, guns drawn. But there was no one to shoot, no one to arrests. Tina's killer lay motionless on the living room floor.

Sara Sue had to suppress the smile that threatened to break out on her face. She had gotten him. It may have been in a roundabout way, it may have fallen in her lap and almost killed her, but in the end, she had gotten him. She couldn't bring Tina back, but she did the next best thing: she put the bastard that killed her out of commission.

She and Charlie were taken to the back of an ambulance to receive oxygen. Their neighbors were out in full force, watching the spectacle. She couldn't blame them; the most activity they ever had in their neighborhood was a loud party every now and then. This was sensational. A fire. A murder. Two people in an ambulance. How could you miss it?

"I love you, Sara Sue. With everything that I am."

Charlie's voice was hoarse and choppy, but it sounded beautiful to her. Tears welled in her eyes as she hugged him, holding on for dear life.

She whispered in his ear, "I love you to, Charlie. More than you know." She let that sink in before continuing, "I'll tell you everything. You deserve to know the truth."

She didn't know why she said it. She didn't have to tell him—all the evidence was gone; the killer was dead. The whole thing was over. But she felt she had to. It was time to start fresh, and that meant leaving all the garbage in the past. This was part of it, and if she and Charlie were ever going to work, she had to get this out of their way.

Charlie squeezed her tighter and said something she didn't expect. "I don't care about any of it, Sara Sue. All I want is to know that you love me."

Sara Sue pulled away far enough to look at him. He was being sincere, meant every word he said. After everything that had happened, Charlie loved her and would be there for her, come what may. She didn't know what she had done to deserve a love like that.

Sara Sue looked at Charlie as if seeing his face for the first time. There was pain in his eyes. She had put it there. She planned to do everything she could to erase it.

She took off her oxygen mask, then his, and kissed him on the lips. Nothing long, just a nice, soft peck. She put their masks back on and smiled at him.

"Love isn't strong enough to describe how I feel about you," she said.

She meant it, too.

EPILOGUE

EPILOGUE

One day since she had almost died but didn't.

Zero days until Mars.

Sara Sue donned her new zebra-patterned flip-flops and made her way to the chaise lounge on the hotel patio where iced tea and a telescope awaited her. It was Mars night and she was ready for it. Sara Sue and Mars were kindred spirits, both fighting for rebirth, both fighting to be seen. Without Mars, she wouldn't be where she was right now.

They were staying at a swanky hotel in town. After they left the hospital and finished up at the police station, they decided to treat themselves. Nothing like a near-death experience to make you see things differently, right? They had never stayed in such a fancy place—there was marble in the bathroom, a bidet that they planned to try, and a big, comfy bed.

They had already tried that out.

Sara Sue didn't need her theme music now. She could barely envision Troy's pouty lips forming the words to those dated songs anymore. In fact, she was thinking of giving her Lover CD to Karen, who might get a good laugh out of it, especially if she looked at the cover. She also decided that she didn't care that her toenails were painted fuchsia and not French manicured like the trendy city women. She was being herself, and she loved it.

Charlie came out onto the patio to meet her with his glass of iced tea in hand. The night was beautiful, warm, with a breeze just like they said it would be for most of the week. The sky was so clear they might be able to see Mars with the naked eye.

Sara Sue's stomach fluttered with excitement. Would Mars look red in the night sky, like a big cherry suspended in the darkness? She hoped so; she wore red lipstick, the color of blood, to match it, just in case it did. She cleaned the lens on the telescope for the fifteenth time that night. She wanted to see Mars' rings as clearly as she could. Or was it Jupiter that had the rings? Sara Sue didn't know and she didn't care. Because it didn't matter anyway.

The End

MORE FROM L. MARIE WOOD

A group of friends head out to enjoy a much-deserved night out and paintballing is on the menu. But the team they are playing against has something entirely different in mind. The friends find themselves in a battle for their lives in unfamiliar terrain against well-equipped opponents whose motivations are both irrational and lethal.

Considered, "… a true trip into the darkest depths of what mankind is capable of at its worst," by Midwest Book Review, this story is a classic tale of prey combined with slasher film "edge-of-your seat" vibes with a little modern-day relevance to keep you unsettled.

Blackened Roots is a unique collection and will be a must-have for zombie lovers. Blackened Roots takes the zombie mythos back to its roots. Drawing from a variety of cultural backgrounds, Blackened Roots imagines a world of horror and wonder where Black protagonists take center stage – as zombies, as hunters, as heroes. From a haunting recipe to sibling rivalry, a singing zombie cowboy, a slave ship, and disobedient gods stories, Blackened Roots is a groundbreaking Afrocentric zombie anthology celebrating the rich cultural heritage of the African Diaspora.

Patrick thought he knew what awaited him in the afterlife. He's learning the hard way that he was dead wrong. He is hunted by a race of giant beasts, the likes of which have never been seen by living eyes, and he is surrounded by the newly-dead from worlds beyond knowing. In this Realm, nothing and no one can be trusted.

Patrick's choices will create echoes in the world of the living. He may be the key to salvation in this Hell known as The Realm, but it may come at the cost of his family.

With his legacy on the line, can he make the right choice?

https://www.mochamemoirspress.com

ABOUT THE AUTHOR

L. Marie Wood creates immersive worlds that defy genre as they intersect horror, romance, mystery, thriller, sci-fi, and fantasy elements to weave harrowing tapestries of speculative fiction. She is the recipient of the Golden Stake Award, a MICO Award-winning screenwriter, a two-time Bram Stoker Award® Finalist, a Rhysling nominated poet, and an accomplished essayist. Wood has won over 50 national and international screenplay and film awards. Wood has penned short fiction that has been published in groundbreaking works, including the anthologies *Sycorax's Daughters* and *Slay: Stories of the Vampire Noire*. She is also part of the 2022 Bookfest Book Award winning poetry anthology, *Under Her Skin*.

Her nonfiction has been published in Nightmare Magazine and academic textbooks such as the cross-curricular, *Conjuring Worlds: An Afrofuturist* Textbook. Her papers are archived as part of University of Pittsburgh's Horror Studies Collection. Wood is the founder of the Speculative Fiction Academy, an English and Creative Writing professor, a horror scholar with a Ph.D. in Creative Writing and an MFA in Speculative Fiction, and a frequent contributor to the conversation around the evolution of genre fiction. Learn more about L. Marie Wood at www.lmariewood.com.

About Mocha Memoirs Press

Established in July 2010, Mocha Memoirs Press's mission is to amplify marginalized voices in speculative fiction genres (science fiction, fantasy, horror). We publish bold, fearless fiction that pushes boundaries and smashes gatekeepers.

We invite you to review our catalog to review the diversity in our stories. You can access the catalog at https://www.mochamemoirs press.com. Join our newsletter **here.**

<u>You can also find us online:</u>
  Instagram - @mochamemoirspress
  TikTok- @mochamemoirspress
  BlueSky- @mochamemoirspress.com
  Twitter (X)- @mochamemoirspress
  Facebook facebook.com/MochaMemoirsPress

www.ingramcontent.com/pod-product-compliance
Lightning Source LLC
Chambersburg PA
CBHW032033310726
48972CB00002B/654